Among Us

PATHWAYS

S.C. Wieczorek

Copyright © 2011 S.C. Wieczorek.

All rights reserved. No part of this book may be used or reproduced by any means, graphic, electronic, or mechanical, including photocopying, recording, taping or by any information storage retrieval system without the written permission of the publisher except in the case of brief quotations embodied in critical articles and reviews.

ISBN: 978-1-4497-1978-4 (e)
ISBN: 978-1-4497-1979-1 (sc)
ISBN: 978-1-4497-1980-7 (hc)
Library of Congress Control Number: 2011932238

WestBow Press books may be ordered through booksellers or by contacting:

WestBow Press
A Division of Thomas Nelson
1663 Liberty Drive
Bloomington, IN 47403
www.westbowpress.com
1-(866) 928-1240

Because of the dynamic nature of the Internet, any web addresses or links contained in this book may have changed since publication and may no longer be valid. The views expressed in this work are solely those of the author and do not necessarily reflect the views of the publisher, and the publisher hereby disclaims any responsibility for them.

Any people depicted in stock imagery provided by Thinkstock are models, and such images are being used for illustrative purposes only.

Certain stock imagery © Thinkstock.

Printed in the United States of America

WestBow Press rev. date: 7/8/2011

Among Us

Chapter 1

OTIUM HAD WATCHED FOR YEARS. Many, many years … with as many years as he had accumulated, most would consider him to be an expert on behavior, but he would never be so bold as to suggest such a thing.

Most people are pretty simple. Their motivations are mostly primal and clearly communicated, many times outright verbally:

"I'm hungry …"

"I'm cold …"

"I'm so sick of this garbage …"

So on and so forth.

Surprisingly though, children were the most difficult to read. Sure, babies were tough, mainly due to their lack of verbal communication, but more often Otium was puzzled by teenagers, especially teenage girls. Although they sometimes carried the physical appearance of adulthood, after periods of observation the insecurity of youth and life experience would usually reveal itself. The confidence they exuded was very often just covering for a strange kind of "uncomfortableness" with themselves. But maybe uncomfortableness was the wrong word. Was it restlessness? Anxiousness? Awkwardness? Maybe all of the above. They had so much energy and passion, and then there were so many moods, emotions and thoughts, all within the span of a very short period of time. It was fascinating, but also difficult to follow along.

Uh-oh, Otium thought. *She's daydreaming again.*

Emily Newhouse was his latest assignment, a seventeen-year-old from South Bend, Indiana. Of all his assignments, he loved the ones that had him working directly with people, especially teenagers. They really kept him on his toes!

He particularly enjoyed Emily. She was smart, kind, a good friend, and a good daughter. Her redeeming qualities far outweighed her "areas for improvement." Beyond that, she was fun to be around. While she took her family, friends and school life very seriously, she didn't get so wrapped up and fixated that she missed out on the best parts. Up until the last few weeks …

Emily needed to be studying but she was staring off into space … What was she looking at now? One minute she was studying and "bopping along" with her MP3 player; the next, she was a thousand miles away. Otium needed to change his vantage point to see what had caught her attention, so he floated alongside her to see what she was staring at.

Aha, he thought, *the prom dress.*

It always annoyed Otium how adults would minimize this time in a teenager's life. The number of events and pressures, comparatively speaking, would drive many grown adults bonkers!

First there was school—involving classes that most adults claimed that they could not handle if they had to retake them. Classes the teens attended at the same time as many of their friends, plus their enemies. Then there was the college applications, the SAT, the entrance exams—and some colleges even required community service. Of course, the application always looked better if you had a few extracurricular clubs and events too, so for Emily, there was the debate team, the math club, the physics club …

It was all so exhausting. As if the pressure of the SATs weren't enough, Emily had been researching colleges and careers. And although it might sound like an unlikely curse, Emily's problem was that she was *too talented*. She excelled at all her school subjects, and that made it much more difficult to choose. As much as it was not something to complain about, Otium thought it was actually easier to choose a career path when your interests and talents were more limited. Unfortunately, Emily's friends and family really didn't offer much help, not that they were trying to make it difficult for her, but the advice they gave was usually not very applicable for her. All too often, humans had a tendency to advise what would be best for them, and not what would be best for the person they were advising.

She's still daydreaming, Otium thought as he looked around the room. *What is she thinking? She's going to kick herself later if she wastes too much time dreaming about the prom ...*

The window was open. He quickly moved between Emily and the window and gently, ever so gently, blew ...

The page to the study guide ruffled a little bit. She was still staring at the prom dress.

Hmmm ...Otium contemplated what to do. The prom was one of the biggest events of senior year, definitely a big distraction, and the dress was just a reminder of that distraction. A reminder that she had a dress and no date, at least not yet. She knew John would call, but he hadn't yet, and that was busting her up inside.

Otium decided to try again. He blew hard. The pages flipped. Emily looked down and sighed, frustrated because she had lost her place. She looked for a paper clip as she flipped back to the page where she had lost her spot and slid the paperclip onto the page. Tying her hair back into a ponytail, she went back to actually studying.

Otium smiled. *Mission accomplished; back on course,* he thought.

Just then he felt a chill. He had never known the actual sensation of cold, but he had learned to recognize the coldness of an empty spirit. The chill that evil brought with it.

From the shadows of the room, Kako slowly emerged.

Chapter 2

"HELLO, OTIUM, MY OLD FRIEND ..." Kako announced.

"Old friend?" Otium asked. "I didn't realize we were friends."

"Don't be such a cliché, Otium," Kako quipped in return. "Of course we are."

Otium had grown to respect Kako, much the way you would respect a dangerous, wild predator. He was intelligent and cunning—and never to be trusted. The classic prototypical demon, he was stunningly impressive on the outside and complete garbage on the inside; basically a spirit devoid of any redeeming qualities. And just as all demons did, he had a way of tangling you up through what seemed to be just casual discussion. Talking with him always seemed to be innocent or harmless at first, but always became confusing and misleading in the end.

Otium knew from many past sparring sessions that he needed to tread carefully.

"A cliché? What do you mean?" Otium asked, cautiously curious.

"We've had our disagreements in the past, but ultimately we are the same. We are just following orders, being the 'dutiful' servant. I can respect that of you, can't you respect that of me?" Kako reasoned.

Otium cringed. "We are *not* the same! What are you up to?"

"Well, that certainly is direct. Why do I have to be up—" Kako paused, feigning levity and freely waving his arms as if he was dancing—"to anything? I just came to visit you. I heard you were here."

Kako strutted around the room, pretending to examine the collectables, ribbons, and photographs Emily had proudly displayed as though he were really interested. Otium watched him carefully. *Never take your eyes off a snake*, he thought. He knew the second he did, there would be trouble.

"By the way, what are *you* doing here?" Kako taunted, eyeing him suspiciously. "What is she, sixteen, seventeen years old? Hardly worthy of the 'Great Otium.'"

"People are my favorite assignments, especially the young ones," Otium lightly replied. "The Boss knows this; that's why He assigned me here. Sometimes it's a refreshing change of pace for me."

"That is vile, Otium. Over the years He has trusted you with so much. And this," Kako lectured, pointing at Emily and her ribbons making an exaggerated face of disgust, "is ridiculous. You should find it insulting. He normally gives these assignments to the less accomplished 'servants.'"

He paused waiting for Otium's reaction, but Otium did not take his bait. After a moment Kako continued, waving his hands around the room again, "Oh, I'm sorry, there I go again. I'm sure you don't appreciate my use of the word 'servant' in this context. That must really be why you're so cranky!"

"I'm not cranky, and I don't mind being a 'servant.' I think you are just trying to get a rise out me, and it's not going to work," Otium replied.

"Well then, what is this new assignment? Is she the virgin that will give birth to the next Christ?" Kako said sarcastically.

"Watch yourself, Kako. You are treading where you shouldn't." Otium shot back.

"Again, my apologies, Otium. I can see that you are especially sensitive today, and I didn't come to fight; this is a social call. I just can't help but wonder why *He* is wasting your considerable talents here." Kako replied innocently. "Is she important?"

"They are all important." Otium quickly replied.

"Hardly … they are like insects," Kako teased.

"They are *all* important!" Otium replied, beginning to lose his patience.

"Well, look." Kako motioned to the prom dress. "I do believe someone is going to a ball." He slid one finger under one of the straps on the hanger and slipped it off. The dress crumpled to the floor.

Emily immediately jumped up and went to the dress to scoop it off the floor. As she did, Kako kicked a bit of the crinoline under the door. As Emily lifted the dress to return it to the hanger, she could hear a few of the stitches rip as it caught on the door.

"Darn it!" she exclaimed. She pulled the dress back down and began searching for the tear.

"Why did you do that?" Otium exclaimed, showing his full annoyance.

"Why are you here?" questioned Kako. "She must be important for Him to have sent you—you, one of His best."

"I don't know why the Boss sent me," replied Otium. "He doesn't always tell me."

"Well, that's got to be annoying. It's not like you're one of the rookies. Come on, Otium … she must be important. That's why He sent *you*."

"I told you, He knows I enjoy taking care of the teenagers! Besides, I don't need to understand the bigger plan," replied Otium. "He dispatched me, and I gladly—"

"You are pitiful," Kako hissed, interrupting Otium in mid-sentence. "How can you just blindly scurry off to do His bidding, year after year, century after century? You are as lost as these pathetic creatures!"

Kako then moved to place himself behind Emily so that she was between the two of them. While Emily could not see the events unfolding around her, Otium could see that she caught a chill as Kako began to summon all the negative evil energy around him. Kako slowly settled into an aggressive crouching posture just a few feet from Emily.

"Stand down, Kako!" shouted Otium.

"*Why?* Who is she?" Kako hissed back.

Emily dropped to her knees holding the dress, frustrated as she searched for the tear.

Using the voice that had once brought down the walls of Jericho, Otium shouted, *"She is in my charge, and you will stand down!"* His voice boomed, shaking the spirit realm.

Kako twisted his body and crouched lower to the ground as though he was preparing to pounce. He drew one arm behind him, coiled and ready to strike. *"Who is she? Why is she so important?"* he loudly hissed again.

Otium was now angry and widened his footing, preparing himself for the impending confrontation. He did not know Emily's importance, her position or her future, but he did know that at the very least she was loved and it was his job to protect her. She was entrusted to him and he would defend her to the end. Raising his fists into a fighting stance, he could feel the Lord's Power swelling within him.

"She is no one, just a girl. And if you touch her, I will strike you down … here—and—now!" He screamed each word at Kako with all his might.

Then suddenly, as if he had flipped a switch, Kako changed his demeanor. He stood up straight and dropped his aggressive stance toward Emily, taking a few steps away from her. "That's all I wanted," Kako calmly replied. "You said it … she is no one. I knew it." And as sleekly as he had entered the room just moments ago, he began his exit.

"What?!" Otium shouted, still charged and ready. "That's not what I meant! She is very—"

"I knew she was no one, no one at all, just one of God's pathetic little creatures," Kako spryly interrupted, "and you said it yourself." Smiling brightly, he guiltlessly glided out of Emily's room through the exterior wall.

Otium had never felt adrenaline (as he was not created that

way), but from what he had seen, this was the same kind of rush. His hands shook, as he realized the whole purpose of the encounter was to get a rise out of him—and it worked. And although Emily was oblivious to all that had just happened, she sat on the floor and began to cry, holding the ripped dress.

"I'm such a klutz," she whispered, as the tears rolled down her face. "I can't take any more of this! The SAT, finals, my dress is messed up, and on top of it all, John still hasn't called. I just can't handle this anymore." She threw herself across her bed and began sobbing.

Otium felt horrible. Once again Kako had slithered in, and right before his eyes, with what seemed to be a few minor steps, thrown everything into chaos. Otium sat down next to Emily on her bed.

"I'm so tired of this!" she cried.

Otium gently wrapped his wings around her and whispered in her ear, "Sleep …"

For a moment, Otium thought she had actually heard him as she stopped crying and looked around the room as though she had heard something. Then after wiping the tears from her face, she lay down on her bed, staring at the ceiling, blinking her eyes slowly as they were heavy with fatigue. Finally after several minutes, she closed her eyes and fell into a restful sleep.

Otium also began to slowly relax as he sat on the bed next to her. He felt the familiar warmth of the Boss's presence welling up within his chest as he reached out to reconnect with Him. It was like the pleasant feeling of walking outside and feeling the sun on a crisp spring day. As Otium re-centered himself, he heard, as though from everywhere around him, "It's okay, Otium … you did well."

His words always made everything right.

Chapter 3

OTIUM PONDERED WHAT HAD JUST happened. Over the centuries, he had had many interactions with Kako. Sometimes playful, sometimes confrontational... but always painful in some way. Somehow the result always ended with someone getting hurt. Kako was a volatile creature, unpredictable, and that was very unsettling to Otium. He always had a difficult time understanding the nature of Kako's kind, their past... why they acted as they did... how and why they were so devious. All Otium could imagine was that they were the "yen" to his kind, the opposite in all the ways that counted.

Otium was a Seraph, an angel of the order Seraphim, and the Boss had created his kind with all the brilliance of the stars, as beings of His Light. His Glory flowed through them like a conduit, and they were the tools for carrying out His work. When the Fallen decided to turn their backs on Him, they became the absence of that Light as He left them; like the black holes of the universe, their primary occupation became the consumption of everything good around them. All that was left of their former selves was the handsome outer shell that He had originally created ... when their dark, bitter insides were not shining through. They became the "dark ones" or demons, and they spent every waking hour seeking out ways to ruin anything the Boss had created.

The expertise Otium had acquired from centuries of observing humans hardly carried over to understanding Kako's dark soul. Kako often surprised him, and despite the damage he left in his wake, Otium would still speak with him, even though the conversation was always strained and full of suspicion. Deep down, even with all the damage that had occurred at Kako's hands, Otium still saw him as a rebellious brother who had lost his way—someone so lost, or even delusional, that he no longer remembered the truth of the way things were, only the lies and paranoid fantasies that he constructed in his own mind.

Emily stirred a little. Otium looked at the clock and decided to let her sleep a little longer. Today was the big test day, the SAT, and the rest would do her more good than a few extra minutes of studying.

Otium's mind drifted back to Kako. Could there be some way to help Kako remember the grand days when he was happy to serve? Thinking back to the first time they had met, Otium just shook his head in disgust. It was unfortunate on many fronts...

Otium at that point in his existence had never witnessed human warfare in the literal sense, and he was not quite sure what to expect. In the millennium before humanity, he had participated and was even a leader in some of the most important conflicts in all of history. He had himself been tested in battle many times, and yet he felt something he never had before; after centuries of reflection, he would now describe it as a feeling of anxiousness.

Otium had heard that human conflicts were much more primitive and savage than the warfare he had known, but there was also something more animalistic as well. There was a ferociousness and brutality to human conflict that was required, because to bring about a physical death, one had to disrupt or stop the physical flow of life through another being's body. Therefore, physical warfare, especially hand-to-hand combat, had an element of feverishness, as masses of opponents race to overcome one another in a chaotic clash.

As Otium came onto the scene, he first observed Moses away from everyone on a hill, talking to a younger man. That man was Joshua, and he was to be Otium's next assignment. Joshua was a young man, strong and brave but untested as a leader. Otium was only told that Joshua would be the leader of this young nation and was pivotal in many future plans. Moses now had both his hands on Joshua's shoulders, and they both bowed their heads. Otium felt the familiar warmth inside himself as Moses prayed. He glanced about, and all the other Seraphs that had assembled looked at each other, feeling His presence too. The anxiousness that Otium had felt earlier was now gone.

Moses was then joined by his brother, and Joshua left them and ran down the hill. He was shouting to the men to lift their spirits, but Otium paid no attention to that. His attention was drawn to the opposing force that was approaching. It was far superior in numbers, and there was something else, something more disturbing: there were many "dark ones" scattered among them.

These people were called the Amalekites and were especially evil. They would rape and pillage neighboring tribes, making their living off the backs of others. And now Otium understood why; if they were always in the "counsel" of so many dark spirits, their unnatural and dishonorable ways would look like a common and normal way to live.

Within seconds the two forces were running directly at each other, without hesitation. Both sides knew why they were meeting in this place. It was as Otium had been told, very violent, chaotic and disorganized. At times, he could hardly tell who was fighting whom. It was then that he first saw Kako.

All the dark ones had a kind of beauty, but Kako was somehow more impressive. Otium had heard human women talk about the magnetic draw of a "bad boy", or the way men would describe a muscle car as cool, and Kako seemed to have both these qualities. But it was the way Kako moved that interested Otium;

he was quick, forceful, and deliberate. Completely committed to his actions; he brought a nefarious agility to his every move. Somehow the combination of all these qualities made him one of the scariest demons Otium had ever seen, as Kako had the potential to play the part of the skilled trickster, the earnest con man or the deadly warrior with ease.

Kako was running next to Kelam, one of the Amalekite leaders. As they ran through the battle, Kako would grab Kelam by the shoulders and twist him toward Kako's choice of prey. The disturbing point of this was that Kako's targets were always engaged with another soldier, and Kelam had no qualms toward plunging his blade into the back of another man. As Otium watched, he became more and more repulsed but was unsure what to do. He was there to observe his next charge, but surely it was not to ignore the injustice of the bigger picture around him.

Otium believed that while it was difficult to observe any conflict where the goal was the death of another, it was somehow more palatable if it contained elements of a one-on-one matchup or a balanced fight. There needed to be at least a basic level of respect or honor for an opponent in battle, even if they were one's most hated foe. Kako and Kelam's actions violated these basic tenets, and as this dishonorable engagement continued, Otium could feel his earlier anxiousness returning.

It was then that Otium realized that Kelam and Kako were making their way toward Joshua, and this realization came to him as a "call to duty." Beyond feeling the need to correct the injustice before him, Otium had already felt an intense bond of protective loyalty toward Joshua. For Otium, once the Boss entrusted someone to him, there was no greater duty, and he would even sacrifice himself before allowing his charge to be hurt.

He sprang from his post and down to the battlefield where it was complete chaos as he ran among the men engaged in battle. The intense struggle raged all around him and was literally the physical manifestation of the battle between good and evil. In every direction he looked, there was evidence of a desperate struggle for Joshua's men to stop the advance of the Amalekites, to protect their homes and families from these people, and to make sure that they would not return to try again.

Otium reached Joshua just in time, and grabbing Joshua's sword arm he spun him around, exposing Kelam's cowardly attack from behind. Out of reflex, Joshua immediately raised his sword, blocking what would have been a hacking slice across the soft part of his back.

As the two men clinched in the heat of battle, Otium turned his attention to Kako.

"What is the meaning of your interference in this human matter, you dishonorable coward?!" Otium shouted.

"Is it only I who am interfering here?!" Kako shouted back, pulling a large-headed battle hammer from a strap on his back.

"How dare yooou ..." Otium shouted as he was interrupted by the hammer striking him solidly in the chest. The blow sent him careening backward, causing a massive shock wave that violently shook the ground, unbalancing all the nearby battling humans. They were thrown every which way as Otium flew uncontrollably backward through them.

As a seasoned warrior, Otium had developed the discipline and sheer will to enable himself to power through this kind of pain. Warfare in this realm was directed to disrupt the energy of his spirit, and he had to shake off Kako's attack and recover, as it would only be a mere fraction of a second before Kako would be on him again.

Otium rolled back to his feet, drawing his sword in one smooth, acrobatic motion. The sword glowed brightly as he channeled the Lord's energy through the weapon. As Kako swung again with all his might, Otium swung under him, striking Kako on the hands and sending the hammer flying. The look on Kako's face was one of extreme pain and surprise all at once.

"Who are you?" Otium shouted.

"I am Kako!" he screeched, crouching over, clutching his hands in pain. "Remember me, meddler! For the next time we meet, you will be licking your broken wings all the way home

to Abba!" And without another word, Kako shot straight up into the air like a rocket, laughing hysterically as he retreated out of sight.

Collecting himself, Otium looked around. A number of Israelites and Amalekites were stunned and dragging themselves to their feet. They had no idea what had just happened in the invisible world around them; only that the ground shook and they were knocked off their feet, by … something. Otium desperately scanned the crowd, searching for Joshua. He knew better than most how much could have transpired in just the few seconds he was distracted while dealing with Kako. Otium sighed with relief as he finally spotted Joshua, standing over Kelam's dead body, breathing heavily with exhaustion from the fight.

Just then Emily stirred again, drawing Otium out of his memories and back to the present. She had not set her alarm as she went to sleep, and there was no way that he was going to let her oversleep on test day. He nudged her a little, then a second time.

She began to wake, mumbling, "I should have stayed up to study …" slapping her hand on her forehead and stretching. She slowly looked around the room as she cleared her head. Rolling out of bed, she dropped to her knees.

"Hello, God. It's Emily. I could really use your help today, if only to calm my nerves …" she began to pray out loud. Then she bowed her head, closed her eyes and continued silently.

Otium smiled. He didn't know what else Emily was discussing with the Boss, but he knew that He was smiling too, because again Otium could feel God's calming peace descending onto the room like a warm summer breeze.

Chapter 4

ONE OF THE PERKS OF this job is definitely the variety, Otium thought, as he sprawled out, completely relaxed, lounging in the backseat of Emily's car. On this morning, she was unusually quiet; no radio, no cell phone. It was, of course, because this was the big day, the SAT, and she had to pick up Jen and get to school *on time.*

As much as Otium considered himself to be an "angel of action," the calm, quiet times in his life were some of the most rewarding. He found that in the quiet times, things would often be revealed to him. The most magnificent was his bearing witness to the formation of a nebula in space. The most philosophical was his own resolution of the classic "Why am I here?" question. And while the revelations were completely different in nature, both were spectacular and had a deep connection to his understanding of "things."

Reflecting back to the nebula, Otium recalled that it took place many millennia ago. The Boss had called a few of His Seraphs together with Him in one of the darkest regions of the heavens that Otium had ever seen. At that time, Otium was not quite sure why the Boss had summoned him; he only had the feeling that it was going to be somehow important. He knew that whenever he was summoned in this fashion, it was because the Boss wanted to share or reveal something to them. On some occasions, the Boss would do everything like a demonstration and leave them to watch, as though He was teaching a lesson. Other times, He directed them to specific tasks, like the conductor of an orchestra directing His team to work together to accomplish His objective. In either case, the Boss was brilliant both as soloist and conductor, and Otium knew that regardless of the role he himself would play, he was in for a treat!

In the dark, absolute silence of space, the Boss began to do His work: manipulating forces, drawing all the once invisible particles together, and then it began … the energy, the colors; it was incredible! Where there was once nothing, He had painted a three-dimensional masterpiece out of ionized gases, spanning a distance of several thousand light years across…

"What do you think, my friends?" the Boss asked.

Otium was awestruck, and nearly speechless.

"It is … *incredible!*" he stuttered with excitement and wonder, struggling to describe his emotions. The others followed suit with similar comments, but Otium didn't really hear them; he was too overwhelmed with the awesome display before them.

"I made it for our enjoyment. And although Man cannot see it now, someday he will …"

It was then that Otium realized one of his most comforting truths: the Boss cared enough to go to the trouble of creating something just to make him happy. He knew that someday His other creations would grow and develop the knowledge to enable them to see the beauty of this nebula. It was then that Otium knew with all his heart that God knew what He was doing…

Jen suddenly bounded into the car and enthusiastically asked Emily, "Are you ready?"

"Well, as ready as I can be," Emily replied. "I'm having trouble focusing a bit. I can't stop thinking about John."

"Are you kidding? John will call—and if he doesn't, then he's lame and doesn't deserve to go to prom with you!" Jen joked, as she tried to comfort her friend. Then changing the subject, she threw up her arms, flexing them like a bodybuilder, and exclaimed, "We are two smart and powerful women! *We are gonna rock the S. A. T!*" The two girls laughed, as Emily carefully backed the car out of Jen's driveway.

A good friend, Otium thought. Emily needed a cheerleader right now, and Jen was doing a good job of it.

"I'm glad you're so confident," Emily said a little sheepishly.

"Emily! We've been studying for weeks," Jen said sternly, "and you're the smartest chick I know. You'll do fine."

"You're right about one thing..." Emily said.

"What's that?"

"If John doesn't ask me to prom, then he *is* lame!" Emily teased, even while she vented some of her annoyance that he hadn't called.

"That's the spirit! Who needs him, anyway?" Jen replied. "Once you ace this thing and get into MIT or Harvard or wherever, you'll invent the next Velcro or something like that, and then you can hire him to clean your pool."

"And he can jealously stare at me as I have six hot guys feeding me grapes, doing my nails, waiting on me hand and foot!" Emily continued the fantasy.

"Exactly!" Jen exclaimed. "On a different note, have you figured out where you're going to apply yet?"

Emily suddenly got an uncomfortable look on her face. "No—I can't decide."

"You know, you don't have to have it all figured out," Jen lectured. "You can apply to schools, without picking a career."

"Well ... yes and no," Emily replied. "If I'm going to pursue the sciences, I'm going to want to head for MIT. But if I'm going to be a lawyer, I think I'd better aim for Harvard or Yale." Emily trailed off and then went silent, as she continued thinking about it to herself.

After a quiet moment, Jen broke the silence, "You know ... it's good to have opportunities, Em. I'll be happy just getting in anywhere."

"I know, it's just so overwhelming. Not knowing what to do, where to go ..." Emily sighed.

"Let's just forget about that for now!" Jen interrupted. "Right now, let's just focus on those grapes by the pool, and the six hot guys!"

"Okay, you can focus on the hot guys; I'm going to focus on the test," Emily teased.

"You're right! " Jen exclaimed. "Test now—grapes and guys later!"

As they hunted for a parking spot at school, the silliness continued, and the girls' mood lightened dramatically. By the time they had parked, you would never have thought that they were on their way into a three-hour college aptitude test. Otium concluded that this was definitely an occasion where Jen was good for Emily. There was a crazy wisdom and truth in Jen's words to Emily: she *didn't* have to have it all figured out now.

Otium had not laughed quite so hard in some time and felt that the Boss must have known that he needed this lighter assignment. As the girls collected their stuff, exiting the car, they continued the silliness as they went inside.

And again, Otium enjoyed the peace.

Chapter 5

KAKO STUCK HIS HEAD IN the car.

"Argh!" Otium sighed. "What are you doing here?"

"Is that any way to greet someone?" Kako replied mockingly. "I thought you were a being of Light, and you loved all creatures—even me!"

"Oh, shut up," Otium said, exasperated. "You can ruin any moment—"

"Aww … were you having a special one?" Kako replied, mocking him again. "I guess you have so few, since you're always slaving away, helping these ridiculous creatures. I'm surprised they figured out how to wipe their own behinds …"

Otium sat quietly, trying to ignore him. He loathed him but had to love him. Over the years they had fought, argued, and debated, and Otium would have been perfectly happy if Kako never came back, but he always did. Maybe someday he would get through to Kako and help him to understand, to remember, and to realize that he had made a mistake—but Otium had never known any of their kind to admit their mistakes.

"Don't you get tired of it?" Kako asked.

"Tired of what?" Otium replied, his attention returning back to Kako.

"Look at you. You are one of the magnificent ones, and you

are stuck here, dealing with the amebas of this world. A thankless job, if you ask me." Kako declared, while expressing as much contempt as he possibly could.

"Kako, don't you remember what it was like?" Otium said, redirecting the conversation.

"What are talking about?" Kako looked genuinely surprised.

"Before the expulsion, before the rebellion," Otium said, trying to ignite the old memories.

"Hah! Of course I remember," Kako said sarcastically, but as he did, the expression on his face suddenly changed. As much as Kako tried to maintain his arrogant persona, Otium could see cracks in his hard exterior shell. It seemed to cause him pain just to think about those days, even though he might never admit to it. After a brief pause, Kako continued, but he was now acting less confident as he stared blankly off into space. "Always being ordered around. Working on menial tasks. Wasting my time on His bidding. Now I do what I want to do ..."

Just then the girls returned from taking the test, jabbering on excitedly. As they hopped into the car, they continued discussing the ordeal. Suddenly Jen blurted out, "Let's go shopping! After all, we deserve it. We need to celebrate!"

"Not a bad idea," Emily replied. "I could use some non-thinking, non-studying, non-scheduled—time off!"

Emily carefully backed her mom's car out of its parking spot and exited the school lot to the main road.

"This! This is exactly what I'm talking about!" Kako exclaimed, pointing at the girls. "How can you let Him order you to waste your time like this?"

"I'm not wasting my time," Otium said, shaking his head in disagreement.

"They're mindless! Shopping—*shopping* is important to them!" Kako said, raising his voice an octave.

"Kako, you're wrong. They are much deeper than that; they are just trying to relax," Otium began to explain. "And this is good for me, too. God knows how all the pieces fit together. He knows you, He knows me. Every creature has a purpose, and when we are fulfilling it, we are content ... we are satisfied."

"You've gone crazy," Kako calmly declared. "I've had too much fun at your expense, and now you've completely lost it—"

"No, Kako. The work I do … I enjoy it. He always knows this, He knows what I need, and I know that the tasks He gives me are all part of a bigger picture," Otium explained.

After a long, uncomfortable pause, Kako whispered, "I hate you."

"No, you don't," Otium said, looking into his eyes.

Otium stared at him, trying not to think the worst. These were the times when his kind would suddenly lash out. It was part of who they were. Otium wanted to trust Kako; he wanted to believe that this time would be different.

"This is rubbish," Kako said and then paused. He actually looked as if he was considering what Otium had said.

Am I getting through to him? Otium thought. *That would be incredible.*

Kako stared back at Otium. Then he looked away toward the girls. "They are so pathetic," he hissed.

Just then, Emily's phone started beeping. She was receiving a text.

"Hey, Jen, check out my phone. Did I just get a text?" Emily asked, as she pointed to her backpack. "My phone is in the front pocket of my backpack."

"They are so easy to play off each other …" Kako said slowly, his eyes narrowing as he looked back at Otium.

Otium looked at him, puzzled. *Where is he going with this?*

Jen pulled Emily's phone out of the pocket and looked at it.

"OMG!" she exclaimed. "It's John!"

"Let me see! Let me see!" Emily said excitedly, barely containing herself.

Just then Otium put the pieces together. He looked out the windshield and saw a woman stepping out to cross the street, pushing a stroller, on her phone, and not paying attention to her surroundings.

Otium then looked back to Emily, who was clearly distracted, looking at the tiny text message on the tiny screen of her phone.

"You!" Otium roared.

"Have fun!" Kako chirped, bailing out of the car. "Bye-bye now!"

Even if this was considered an accident, Emily's life would be, at the very least, changed forever. The consequences of this mere fraction of a moment of irresponsibility would affect Emily, Jen, the young mother, and, most assuredly, the infant in the stroller.

Otium looked up. *"Father,"* he screamed. *"Help me!"* And diving forward, he launched his body *through* the front of the car.

At that same moment, Emily glanced forward, realizing what was transpiring. Panicked, she slammed on the brakes, but it was too late. The car was already in the process of striking the stroller and the young mother.

As Otium passed through the car, he stretched his arm forward, reaching for the baby. Through the bumper of car and through the stroller he reached, straining to slide his hand under the infant's body. Then, with all that was left within him, he flicked his wrist, sending the child out of the stroller and into the air.

While Emily's car had begun to slow down as she frantically jammed on the brakes, it was still moving pretty fast as it struck the stroller. The combination of the car's mass plus its speed propelled the stroller diagonally towards an oncoming car. The unsuspecting driver tried to avoid the obstacle, but he, too, struck the stroller, completely destroying it as it was pulled under the car's wheels.

As Emily's car continued moving forward, Otium landed on the pavement behind it in its wake and rolled onto his back—just in time to feel the baby land on his chest, and then gently and transparently pass through him as though it had landed on a pillow.

Crying uncontrollably, the baby was startled but unhurt. Otium's toss was just enough to clear the impact of Emily's car. And as Otium lay on the pavement, he sighed with relief. He looked up to Heaven and whispered, "Thank you."

Chapter 6

THE ACCIDENT SCENE WAS COMPLETE chaos, as Otium assessed what needed to be done. Emily was running toward him, or more accurately to the baby, who was lying unharmed on the pavement next to him. She picked up the child and inspected him for a moment, trying to determine if he was injured, and then rushed off toward the infant's mother.

Jen had jumped out of the car to aid the young mother. The car had struck her but had only clipped her leg. From Emily and Jen's vantage point, it looked as though somehow she had been able to dive away from the car at the very second it was about to strike her. The intense expression of misery was all over her face as she clutched her leg, while sobbing from the pain and screaming for her baby. Emily ran to her and handed her the child. The young mother immediately calmed down as she inspected her little treasure, looking for injuries.

"Thank God," she sobbed, hugging the baby. "He's okay … it's a miracle!"

Otium then saw his old friend Cidem, who was crouching over the mother examining her injuries. He rushed over to them.

"Cidem! It's great to see you," Otium said with relief, hugging his old friend. "Is she going to be all right?"

"It is great to see you too!" Cidem replied happily and then turned back to the young mother and took a closer look at her leg. "I think she is going to be okay. I got here as quick as I could and tried to yank her out of the way, but I was still just a little too late. The car still hit her in the leg, and it looks like she may have a fractured femur." Cidem said with disappointment, as he continued to concentrate on her leg, and then began to look her over from head to toe.

"Cidem, you did a great job," Otium reassured his friend. "If you hadn't gotten here just in time, she would've been toast." He began examining the young mother as well but knew that his areas of expertise were not related to triage or human anatomy.

Over the centuries, the Boss had decided to develop particular skills in each of His Seraphim. Initially, Otium had assumed it was for delegation purposes, but later he realized it was much deeper than that. Ultimately, the Boss needed no one's help; He could handle everything Himself if He wanted to, but in His wisdom He knew that everyone in His charge felt a special satisfaction when carrying out His missions. As the Boss began developing specialties among them, the missions became even more satisfying, as each of them used the special skills and secrets He had shared with them to carry out their very difficult assigned tasks.

Within minutes, an ambulance arrived, as well as a police car. One of the paramedics began tending to the injured mother, while the other assessed the baby to determine the extent of his injuries, if there were any at all. In an attempt to help, Emily and Jen began interjecting what they thought were pertinent facts that the paramedics would require, but the police officer quickly stepped in and instructed the girls to back away so the professionals could do their work unhindered. Once the work area for the paramedics was secured, he pulled Emily aside so that he could begin to unravel the details of the accident.

"Cidem, I've got to go," Otium said. "Emily might need me. Can we talk later?"

"Of course," Cidem replied. "We need to catch up. It's been a long time. I'm just going to hang out here, and then I'll go to the hospital with Sharon and little Mitch."

Otium looked at him, puzzled. "Who?"

"That's their names," Cidem said, smiling and pointing at the young mother, who was now cradling the infant and humming to him as she was tended to on a stretcher. "I'll catch you later. You go take care of Emily!"

Otium walked over to Emily and the officer who was preparing to begin his accident report.

"I'm Officer Stanford," he announced as he pulled out his pen and pad. "I need to see your driver's license and registration, and then we'll run through the details of the accident."

Emily fumbled around in her backpack for a few moments before finally producing the required documents. As Officer Stanford copied the pertinent information into his report, she stood silent and motionless, waiting for him to begin. Although she looked outwardly calm, Otium could tell by her body language and from the hours upon hours that he had spent with her that she was far from calm.

"Okay, Emily, from the beginning. What happened?" Officer Stanford asked.

"Jen and I just finished taking the SAT, so we were driving down this road, heading for the mall. From out of nowhere, this lady was suddenly in the middle of the road with her baby," Emily reported, in a very adult and businesslike tone.

"So she was crossing in the middle of the road, not at the crosswalk?" Officer Stanford asked.

"Yes. It all happened so fast. I don't think she was paying attention," Emily said, sympathetically shaking her head.

"Did you see her look before she crossed?"

"Well"—Emily nervously paused—"I don't know."

"Was your view of her obscured by the parked cars?" Officer Stanford continued.

"I'm not sure," Emily slowly replied, now staring at her shoes.

Officer Stanford looked up from his note taking and then waited patiently as he read her body language. It was obvious he knew what he was doing. If he waited, he knew Emily would tell him something more, and that something was something she didn't really want to tell.

"Well ..." Emily said again, nervously.

Come on, Emily, Otium thought, standing behind her. *Telling the truth has always worked out best for you.*

"I was waiting for this text from John ... he's my boyfriend—well, not really my boyfriend, but this guy that I really want to go to prom with," Emily began, speaking much faster than before, "and I was waiting, and waiting, and waiting, and then finally I got it." She was now rambling so nervously and quickly that Otium thought there was no way the officer could write fast enough to capture her story (nor would he want to). After a moment of listening, Officer Stanford stopped writing and just began to stare at her.

"The SAT was soooo long, and we were both so stressed, Jen and I—we just wanted to go to the mall ... they have this great kiosk where they make these awesome fruit smoothies with frozen yogurt," Emily continued, speaking at record speeds.

Finally, Otium put his hand on her shoulder, trying to channel his peace into her. "Calm down ..." he gently whispered in her ear.

Officer Stanford's eyes began to glaze over as he just stared at her for another moment and then held up his hand for her to stop talking. Emily abruptly stopped. Then he looked at her very seriously. "Do you realize you could have killed someone today?".

"Yes," Emily said, her eyes welling up with tears.

"A car weighs 3,000 to 5,000 pounds. It can be the most dangerous weapon you'll ever touch—look at what it did to that stroller!" He pointed to the mangled baby stroller, partially sticking out from under the other car.

"I understand," Emily said remorsefully, still trying to contain her emotions.

Officer Stanford paused, staring at his notepad. After probably only twenty seconds that seemed like hours, finally he spoke. "As I see it, she crossed in the middle of the road, without a crosswalk.

I think we can all thank the good Lord that her injuries weren't worse, and the baby looks to be unharmed." He paused again while reviewing what he had written. "I don't think the texting thing is relevant to this report."

Emily began to smile a little, but then he continued with stern authority: "But—you and I both know that it was. You had better learn from this!"

"Thank you, Officer! Thank you! It definitely won't happen again!" Emily gushed.

So he cut her a break, Otium thought, smiling to himself. He was normally pretty strict when it came to matters of justice, but in this case, he knew there were extenuating circumstances. For that matter, he felt that Emily had been set up, used as a pawn in some game that Kako was playing.

What is Kako up to now? he pondered.

Emily rushed over to Jen who was standing next to the ambulance, as Sharon and Mitch were being loaded inside.

"I don't think she has anyone," Jen whispered to Emily, "they aren't trying to call anyone."

"Do you want to go to the hospital with her?" Emily asked.

Just as the words left her mouth, the officer walked up behind them and sternly announced, "I don't think so. You two should not even be involved right now. The paramedics and hospital staff can handle this."

"But she needs our help!" Jen protested

"Listen," the officer said in a lower, hushed tone, "you never know where this could go. Even though it looks like this was mostly her mistake, she could turn around and sue you … or more likely your parents …"

"We just wanted to help. I feel so bad," Emily said sadly.

"Trust me," the officer repeated, "we can handle this." He then turned and walked away.

Both the girls walked back to the car, a little confused, but there was definitely a sense of relief between them. Otium felt proud of the girls on many levels, particularly proud of Emily.

Throughout life, trials would come and go, and the most important thing was how you weathered them. In this case, Emily stuck with honesty, when she could have just omitted the truth. Over the years, Otium had seen many supposedly honorable and powerful men cave under less pressure, and here was his seventeen-year-old "assignment" standing up and doing the right thing when the heat was on.

She is a good kid, Otium thought as he climbed back into the backseat of Emily's car, leisurely propping his feet up to relax for the ride home. *Actually, she's a great kid.*

Chapter 7

BACK AT HOME, EMILY'S MOM rushed up to her as she stepped in the door. "So tell me, how did it go?"

"Oh, Mom!" Emily cried, bursting into tears.

"My goodness, Emily," her mom began sympathetically, "don't cry, sweetie. You can take it again—I'm sure you'll do better next time!"

"Mom, it's not that," Emily said, still crying.

She had held it together the whole way to dropping off Jen. The two had talked a little here and there, but the conversation was definitely short, as both were shaken and thoughtful about what had just transpired. Now that she was home, safe with Mom, the floodgates were opening.

"Mom, I was in an accident!" Emily blurted out.

"Are you okay?" Mom asked, in full concern and protect mode. "Was anyone hurt?"

"Jen and I are okay, but I hit this lady with a stroller and—and a baby," she managed to say between sobs.

"Emily!? How did this happen?" Mom was so shocked that she flopped backward onto the couch as though someone had pushed her. Her eyes began welling up with tears. "A baby? Was it okay?"

"Yes! And the whole thing was totally an accident!" Emily

explained, wiping some of the tears off her face with the arm of her sweatshirt. "And everyone is ... mostly okay. I think the mother might have broken her leg."

"Emily, how did this happen?" Mom again asked, visibly trying to collect herself and stay calm.

"The mother wasn't paying attention, and she just walked right out into the street! She came from out of nowhere!" Emily's tone was becoming more indignant and blaming, although she was still struggling to explain through her tears.

"So it was her fault?" Mom replied, with a very a distressed expression on her face. "She must feel awful to have put her baby in such jeopardy!"

This is where things could go off the tracks, Otium thought. *Tell the whole story Emily, not the edited version.*

Emily slumped down on the couch beside her mom. "Mom—" Emily began and then paused as she gathered the courage to tell the rest of the story. "I was not paying full attention either."

Otium was again proud of Emily as she went on to explain the entire incident to her mom, without omitting a single detail. Her mom took it very well but of course read her the riot act for even trying to read a text while driving.

"The officer was right!" she exclaimed. "And I don't even know where to begin as far as your punishment!"

"You're punishing me?" Emily exclaimed, completely shocked.

"I certainly am. And if you were smart"—Mom paused to take a deep breath—"you'd march straight up to your room without debating me on the psychological strategies and methods for disciplining a child!"

Emily looked at the floor as she struggled to find the right words. "It's just been such a tough day, Mom," she said slowly. "We were just excited to be out and free of that crummy test. I just lost my head for a second."

"I know." Mom muttered under her breath as she stared off into space, shaking her head, overwrought with emotion. "Just go up to your room... I need to talk to your dad about this."

"Okay," Emily said soberly and obediently turned to go up to her room.

"Emily," Mom said, suddenly holding her arms out widely, inviting her into a hug. Emily paused for a fraction of a second and then plunged into her Mom's open, loving arms, hugging her tightly as she let out a little whimper of a sob again.

"Emily … " Mom said as she gently grabbed her face with both hands. "I'm just glad you're okay." She then kissed her daughter on the cheek before releasing her to go up to her room.

That was a tough one, Otium thought, as he followed Emily. He had seen many conflicts between children and their parents, and he was very satisfied with the way this one had ended. It was a testament to the character of each member of this family. Each had treated the other with respect and love, and the lesson was delivered and understood.

Emily closed the door behind her and plopped down on her bed. She was still sniffling from all the tears she had let loose earlier, and the massive release of emotions was exhausting. As she sat on her bed, she looked blankly around the room, staring at random objects as she processed through everything that had happened. Every couple of minutes she would pick a new object to fixate on, stare at it, and let out a sigh. Otium watched helplessly, knowing that sometimes there was nothing he could do except let her deal with this new emotional trauma on her own.

Finally her gaze settled on the prom dress. Otium could see tears start to well in her eyes again, but she held them back. She continued to stare at it for another three to four minutes, and then suddenly her expression changed. She frowned a little but at the same time looked curious as she glanced around for her backpack. She picked it up from where she had dropped it on the floor, and carried it to her bed. She sat down and rummaged through the front pocket. Finding her phone, she pulled it out and looked at it. In all the excitement, she never had actually read the text message; she only had seen that it was from John.

She opened the phone and stared at the tiny screen.

"Hey, Em," it read; "hope you crushed the test! Call me. It's impotant!"

"Hmmph ... he spelled *important* wrong," Emily indignantly said out loud; then shrugged and placed the phone on her nightstand. "Moron; I'm not calling you. You're gonna have to call me!"

Emily stared at the phone for another minute before grabbing her favorite stuffed animal, a fuzzy brown horse. She lay down on her bed with it and continued to stare at her phone, beginning to doze off. Within seconds, she was asleep.

Wow! I think the Spanish Inquisition was less emotional! Otium thought. *I need a break!* This incident had taken a toll on him as well, and he could use a friend. With that, he set out to find Cidem.

Chapter 8

AS CIDEM HAD PROMISED, OTIUM found him at the hospital with Sharon and Mitch.

"So have you been assigned to Sharon for a while?" Otium asked Cidem.

"Nope. The Boss just said, 'Cidem it's time for you to set another speed record. Your buddy needs help; get down there!' So I did," Cidem explained. "I just wish I'd gotten there quicker."

"What are you talking about!? You came out of nowhere!" Otium exclaimed. "I knew you were fast, but I didn't even see you!"

"Are you kidding me? Of course you didn't see me; you had your hands a little full, huh?" Cidem teased.

"Yeah." Otium shook his head and looked down.

He loved the relationship that had developed between him and Cidem. They could joke and clown around like college frat brothers, and when he needed to talk, Cidem could be serious and always had wise counsel.

"Looks like her leg was fractured in two places," Cidem reported, nodding his head. "At first I didn't see it, but once things settled down, I got a real good look at it. There was a hairline fracture running lengthwise as well ... tough to see. Fortunately, the doctor ordered a couple of extra pictures, so I think he should catch it as well. They are just waiting for him to get back."

"That is impressive, Cidem. Your skills have really developed!" Otium said in amazement.

"Yeah, He's really been coaching me." Cidem looked upward, pausing. Then a grin spread across his face. "But don't get me wrong… I still enjoy getting a little old-fashioned-style action, kicking it into warp drive and blazing in for a rescue!"

They sat for a moment quietly watching Sharon adjust her "cuddle" on Mitch.

"This kind of work really brings me a lot of joy too, though. It really is amazing the way He designed the human body to function. It's an awesome machine!" Cidem said, still smiling from his earlier comment. "So you said you wanted to talk?"

"Yeah," Otium replied, looking very distracted.

"Well, let's go for a walk and you can tell me what's going on," Cidem said.

"Okay," Otium said with a sigh.

Otium did not know where to begin. This whole mess with Kako was really getting to him. He knew that ultimately it was Kako's nature to be a pest and cause havoc whenever possible, but he just didn't understand what the endgame was. Was he after Emily? Was he just trying to hurt Sharon or Mitch? Was it just totally random mayhem? Or—

He stopped walking, while Cidem continued on for a couple of steps. Cidem, realizing his pal stopped suddenly, turned around.

"Otium, what's wrong?"

Otium suddenly felt very sick. Were Kako's attacks targeting *him?*

"Otium!" Cidem said loudly. "*What* is going on?"

"Oh, Cidem," Otium said, exasperated, "I think these bad things that have been happening lately have been my fault."

"What?" Cidem replied, looking a little surprised. "Come on, Otium—what are you talking about?"

"It's Kako. He's been showing up a lot lately, even before I started watching over Emily. He shows up, and we chat for a bit, and then he makes a mess of things." Otium spoke more and more slowly, as though he were figuring out a puzzle as he spoke. "Not all the time ... and not always serious; sometimes it's just mischief, but like today—today was serious."

"What do you mean, 'We chat for a bit'?" Cidem said, suspiciously curious.

"He talks to me. Most of the time he teases or ridicules me about our work, but sometimes we actually talk about things ... serious things." Otium explained.

"What kind of things?" Cidem said, sounding slightly shocked.

"Well—like just before the accident," Otium said earnestly. "I was trying to get him to remember what things were like before the rebellion, and I think I was actually getting through to him. The expression on his face changed for just a few seconds as he was thinking back to those days."

They walked together silently through the hospital halls. One of the things Otium valued about his friend was that he would really listen; really consider what was being said before responding.

"Otium, look here," Cidem finally said, motioning into one of the long-term care rooms. "This woman, she has a terrible case of arthritis in her hands, among other things ..."

In the room, an elderly woman sat in her bed, slightly elevated, trying to knit. Otium could see the pain on her face as she desperately tried to knit another row.

"Do you know what she is doing?" Cidem asked Otium.

"She's knitting."

Cidem stared at him for a moment and then shook his head. "Yes, of course she is knitting. We can both see that," he said, a bit sarcastically. "I mean, do you know why?"

Otium shrugged. "To make a blanket for someone, I guess."

"Yes, she makes blankets and quilts and then sends them to soldiers in Iraq." Cidem said as he reached out and put his hands transparently inside hers. As Cidem looked up, the Boss's healing warmth began to rain down on them both, bathing everything around them in His Light. The spot where their hands met glowed like the sun for a moment and then slowly faded as Cidem released her hands. Instantaneously, they both could see relief wash across her face, and she began to smile as she continued to knit, but now just a little quicker.

"I think He will take her tonight … her liver is failing," Cidem said. Otium nodded.

"Something kind of interesting here applies to your situation," Cidem explained. "Here is a woman, with the best of intentions, wanting to do something nice … something kind, for someone she will probably never see. Yet, in doing this deed, the pain she feels is excruciating. All for what? Do you think a soldier in the desert really wants a blanket?"

"Sometimes it gets cold in the desert," Otium quipped back, smirking.

"Yeah, sometimes it does … but I think you know what I mean," Cidem said, sounding a little fatherly.

"Yes, I do know what you mean," Otium retorted. "The soldiers probably don't want it and don't need it."

"Right. Ultimately she does it because it makes her feel better," Cidem explained. "She feels good about doing something for someone else." He was sounding more like a psychology professor than an angel.

"Well, I understand your point, but I don't think I exactly agree. Sometimes the effort that people see or experience when you do something for them is the trigger that makes them realize that things can be different, that they should be different, and they change because of it," Otium rationalized.

"Otium—what are you trying to accomplish? Are you really trying to turn Kako?" Cidem asked patiently.

"I don't know." Otium's troubled and earnest tone sounded even to him as if he was trying to convince himself at the same time. "Cidem, once he was like us. They were all like us …"

Both of them stared at the ground sadly, as though they were paying respects at a funeral. At that same moment, the old woman began humming happily as she continued to knit.

Chapter 9

THE TWO STOOD THERE SILENTLY for quite a while, both pondering the conversation and the opposing points that each had just presented.

"Otium," Cidem said suddenly, "can you remember even one of them ever changing sides?"

Otium quietly contemplated Cidem's question. There had been so many interactions with them, so many conflicts. He understood where Cidem was headed.

"No … I don't," Otium replied slowly. "You would think that at least one of them would have changed their minds, reconsidered their decision, something … They must know how things will end."

"Otium, something happened to them when they rebelled." Cidem looked thoughtful as he spoke. "It's like their hearts went ice cold … All they see is the short term … and what makes them happy, right then … the glory they can bring to themselves."

Otium nodded as Cidem spoke. *Why do I want to help Kako? Why do I want him to change his mind and come back home? Is it just sympathy? Am I just feeling bad for another?*

"Do you think if one were to come to Him and ask if they could come home—do you think He would take them back?" Otium asked.

"In a second," Cidem quickly replied. "But I don't think that would ever happen. It's like I said, something changed when they joined Lucifer. Our lives are about serving, teamwork, caring, and dedication; they are infatuated with themselves and their own beauty. They have completely forgotten who made them, that their beauty was not of their own hands, but of His … and now I think they are just insanely bitter. They think only of themselves and bringing others down with them."

For some reason, these words broke Otium's heart. *Why do I care what happens to Kako?* They did have good, meaningful conversations; conversations that actually strengthened his dedication to the Boss.

"You're right, Cidem. But over all these years, all the time he's spent razzing and hassling and challenging me; he's actually strengthened my resolve and my loyalty. The challenging made me think, and the thinking has helped me choose. And maybe since he helped me choose God, maybe I can help him find God again."

"Otium, you have to realize that—" Cidem paused thoughtfully. "Yes, he challenged you… but he was challenging you in hopes to hurt you, not help you." They were both silent again. Their words hung in the air like smoke, and it wouldn't dissipate.

"Think about all of the encounters we have had with them. They have never ended well. They always try to hurt us … or *them*," Cidem said, motioning to the elderly woman. "Mainly because they know how much it hurts Him. And there have been times when the Boss knew that the best thing to do was to just smite them and anything connected to their evil ways." Cidem's words were firm, but delivered with as much compassion as he could muster for their kind.

Otium was quiet, as he contemplated the words of his friend, silently agreeing with him.

In the early days, things were so much simpler. There was good and evil, and the conflicts were clear and right out in the open. He thought again back to Joshua and one time where the battle lines were undeniably clear.

Otium stood with Joshua, as the Messenger appeared to the young leader to deliver a message from the Boss. Otium had the utmost respect and admiration for those chosen to be Messengers. He was divinely impressive, so much so that Otium himself was left in awe; he could only imagine what was going through Joshua's mind. Out of respect, reverence, and fear, Joshua fell to his knees, as the Messenger stood commandingly before them. Reflecting all the Lord's glory, with a drawn sword that glowed like white-hot metal, he told Joshua of the plan.

Joshua was instructed to march the army around Jericho for six days, once each day. But in the lead position, in front of the entire army, he was to put seven priests with trumpets, marching just before the Ark of God. He was to show the enemy that their God, their Faith, was in charge of this campaign.

By the seventh day, the entire army was getting anxious. Many of the soldiers did not understand why they kept marching around the outside wall of this large city. To them it looked to be a huge waste of energy. And on that day they were to march around the city seven times!

But Otium knew of this city and the evil it had harbored. It had walls that were twenty feet thick, and the city itself was heavily fortified. As Otium marched with the men, he talked with the other Seraphs who would be part of the battle, and they could all clearly see why this place was to be destroyed.

On the top of the walls and in guard towers, in addition to the scores of enemy soldiers, Otium could see legions of dark ones sneering at them and coaxing the inhabitants of the city into the most horrid and despicable acts against themselves and others.

As they finished the seventh pass, Joshua began to yell and motioned to the priests and trumpet players to blow their horns. The sound became louder and louder, and just as Otium thought it had reached its peak, a louder and more deafening wave of sound would erupt from the horns and the troops.

It was then that the Boss spoke to all the Seraphs that he had dispatched to the battle.

"I have allowed them free rein of this region for too long. It will now belong to Joshua and My people! Eradicate the evil ones from this city!" God's voice filled Otium's head, so much so that it drowned out the horns and the yelling from the troops. *"Clear the path that they may claim this city in My name!"*

Otium felt his whole being swell with strength, and he turned to Joshua, focusing every thought he could to insert a message into Joshua's head: *Charge!*

Joshua got the message. He began to run toward the city, screaming, and Otium ran next to him, unleashing his own battle cry. Then he ran ahead of Joshua and yelled to the others, *"Clear the way!"*

The other Seraphs charged in after Otium, shouting as they drew their divine weapons and waved them overhead. The sound was deafening, and the ground began to shake. Otium could see cracks beginning to form in the walls.

The dark ones poured over the walls and down onto the battlefield, intending to meet the Seraphs and the Israelite army before they got to the wall. Otium could see every kind of evil being that ever existed heaving toward them, while the enemy human soldiers stood paralyzed with fear on the wall, unsure whether they should retreat or fight.

Otium yelled to the others, *"Louder!"* and the Seraphs surged forward, screaming and trampling the evil ones, tearing through their bodies, throwing them about like they were rag dolls. Then all those in Otium's battle line ducked their heads into their shoulders and slammed their bodies into the wall.

At that moment, the noise from the horns was louder than ever, and the Seraphs and Israelite army yells reached a fevered pitch—and the wall exploded sending the enemy soldiers and evil beasts flying in every direction! The supposedly indestructible wall had been breached!

Suddenly Otium was jolted back to the present. "Otium," Cidem said, looking at his face. "We have seen some amazing things. Things I can hardly describe with words, and we have seen these people"—Cidem motioned to the elderly woman again—"make incredible changes in their lives. Complete transformations. But—"

Otium shook his head. "I know, Cidem. You are right."

"They will not change," Cidem said desperately, "and if they do, it will not be due to your actions or your words!"

Otium just shook his head in disgust. He knew that Cidem was right; he had been wasting his time. All the times Kako had sat and talked with him, it was not because he wanted to exchange ideas or have real fellowship. It was because he was searching for an opportunity; any opportunity, to strike, to hurt him, to hurt mankind.

He clenched his fists. *No more!*

Chapter 10

By the time Otium had arrived back at Emily's house, she had already settled in for the evening. Looking quite comfortable, she was sprawled out on her bed reading a magazine in her "I 'heart' New York" camisole top and boxer-shorts. Her hair was in a ponytail, and she was kicking her feet back and forth, much the way a cat will flick its tail while it is watching a bird or a mouse. *She must be reading something pretty amusing,* he thought, as he prepared himself to settle in for the evening as well.

He was sure that she would sleep well tonight, with all that had happened over the course of the day. First the SAT, then the accident, then having to explain it all to her mom—there was only one more eventuality: her dad would come home from work, and then she would have to explain the whole thing to him as well.

Suddenly they both heard a light tapping at Emily's window. This was a huge surprise to Emily, as her bedroom was on the second floor, but only a mild surprise to Otium. After thousands of years, very little startled him anymore.

Emily rushed to the window and opened it. "John!?" she exclaimed.

John was clinging to a tree branch and tapping the window with another branch.

"Jen called me and told me what happened, so I rushed over here to see if you were okay!" John said, sounding genuinely concerned.

Otium hoped that John's concern was sincere. Emily had had such a rough day, she really didn't need to add dealing with a creep to her list of accomplishments. And then he saw him, another of the dark ones. This one was lounging on the tree branch next to John.

Otium did not recall this one's name, but he'd seen his type before. He had given this kind a nickname: Charmers. And his hope that this visit was actually a sincere, concerned social call just went out the window that John was climbing in.

"I'm okay," Emily said. "But you can't come in! I think I'm grounded!"

"Are you kidding me?" John retorted. "After the day you've had, your parents are grounding you?" He was half holding the window frame, half holding the tree branch, trying to get himself in through the window. Emily grabbed his arm and helped pull him in.

"John, I'm really glad you came over, but I'm not supposed to have any boys in my room … it's my parents' rules!" she explained. "And I don't need any more bad press today … I still need to talk to my dad about what happened."

The Charmer floated into Emily's room with graceful ease through the exterior wall. "Well, well … what do we have here?" he said, just a little too smoothly, looking Otium up and down. "I didn't know this was going to be a party. I was expecting a little more of an"—he shifted his gaze back to Emily—"intimate rendezvous."

Otium inspected the Charmer, and he himself stood up so that the Charmer could get a good look at him as well. Charmers were always handsome creatures, the embodiment of attractiveness, but in earthly terms, they were kind of "players" and somewhat soft. Otium was basically the opposite, a warrior, and he wanted this one to know that if he stepped over the line, he would be sorry.

John sat down on Emily's bed next to her. "So what happened?" he earnestly asked, still sounding concerned.

Maybe this kid is all right, Otium thought. *After all, he doesn't know that this slime ball is following him around.*

Otium locked eyes with the Charmer. "She's had a rough day," he growled, "and I'm fed up with your kind. So you'd better just move along."

But if his threat affected the Charmer, it didn't register on his face.

"Take it easy, big fella. " the Charmer suavely spoke again. "Like you said, she's had a rough day. Let's just give our boy some room to comfort her a little bit ... It will be fine." The Charmer sat down on the bed next to Emily across from John.

Emily nervously recounted the story of the accident to John, and to Otium's surprise, John attentively listened. Otium cautiously thought through the situation. He did not want to overreact. Otium had no reason not to trust John, except that he was a teenage boy—and teenage boys do not always make the best decisions when in the company of cute teenage girls ... especially cute teenage girls in their pajamas.

Then it happened.

As Emily was explaining the details, she was waving her hands around excitedly. The Charmer, seeing his chance to cause a little mischief, pushed the magazine she was reading off the bed and onto the floor. To Emily and John it would have looked as if it slid off due to all the wild motions from her energetic "hand-talking", but Otium could see the Charmer's intentions. As Emily quickly bent over to pick up the magazine, her camisole opened slightly, exposing a small bit of her cleavage to John.

Emily thought nothing of it and continued her story, but to John ... it was as though he'd been hypnotized. He sat there staring at her chest, and it was clear to Otium that the boy's concentration had left him. The wheels were turning in his head, and he wasn't focused on Emily's story anymore.

The Charmer then leaned over, whispered something into John's ear, and then slyly grinned at Otium.

Without any clue or warning, John suddenly reached over to Emily and put his hand on her cheek. Then he leaned forward and gently kissed her on her lips. It happened so quickly that it took her completely by surprise and muted her halfway through a very expressive sentence.

Otium had nothing against young love and kissing; but not while she was in her pj's, in her bedroom, and already on the verge of a grounding. Otium leaped forward. "Okay, time to leave, pal!" he yelled to the Charmer.

"Aww, come on, they're just kissing a little bit," the Charmer innocently protested.

If Otium could have had adrenaline pumping through his veins—or for that matter, if he'd had veins—it would have been happening then. He had had enough of the Charmer. He grabbed him by the neck with one hand and seized a leg with the other, picking him up as though he were made of feathers, and flung him out of Emily's room through the wall by which he had originally entered. Otium threw him with such force that Emily and John felt it rattle in the physical world too, ceasing their kiss to look around.

From Emily's perspective, John's unexpected and somewhat romantic kiss was a little like a daydream suddenly coming true, but was she now experiencing an earthquake too? Indiana didn't have earthquakes, did it?

She looked up just in time to see a very unwelcome surprise for John on its way down from the shelf overhead. Although she was always very proud of the size of her first place horseback riding trophy, she knew this was not going to end well. She closed her eyes just as the trophy landed heavily on John's head.

"Crap!" John yelled, grabbing the top of his head.

"Hmmmm," Otium said, glancing out the window to see the Charmer, looking a little worse for wear, hanging upside down in the tree outside. "That's a funny place for a party," he said, taunting the Charmer.

Suddenly, Emily heard heavy footsteps coming up the stairs.

"Ahhh! My dad is home!" she said, in a panicked half whisper. "Get out!"

She grabbed John by the arm and dragged him back to the window.

"Can't I get an ice pack or something?" John whined. "My head is killing me! I'm going to have a huge lump!"

"You don't understand, the lump on your melon won't matter if my dad catches you up here!" Emily frantically whispered.

John had one leg through the window and was grasping a branch with one hand, when Emily's dad knocked at the door.

"Emily … can I come in?"

"Wait!" John whispered, holding his hand up to Emily's face. "I've got to ask you something."

Emily looked at the door and then nervously back at John. *"What?"*

"Will you go to prom with me?" John whispered.

"Yes!" Emily excitedly yelled as she pushed him the rest of the way out of the window. John landed with a thud on the ground below.

Emily's dad entered her room, thinking that the yes was meant for him.

"What's going on in here?" he asked, looking around the room. "What was all that racket?"

"Oh, my trophy just fell off the shelf," she replied, trying not to sound too nervous.

"Sweetheart!" He grabbed her and hugged her tightly. "I heard you had an eventful day."

"Daddy—you don't know the half of it." She sighed, snuggling into her dad's warm embrace.

Wow! She got that right! Otium thought. *Neither of you know the half of it!*

Otium again looked out the window, this time at poor John trying to catch his breath, lying in the bushes below. Then he looked for the Charmer, who by then had straightened himself and was already sauntering down the street, abandoning John to go make trouble elsewhere.

Cidem was right. This was their nature: no loyalty, no honor, and they didn't care who got hurt. The hurt, in fact, was their goal.

Otium floated down to John, who was still wrestling around in the bushes. He grabbed John by the torso and gently helped him out. *He's not a bad kid, he's just got some bad acquaintances,* he thought as he looked down the street in the direction of the Charmer, who was already long gone and out of sight.

It has been an eventful day, Otium thought as he watched John slowly gather himself and head for home.

Chapter 11

OTIUM REJOINED EMILY AND HER father back in her room. He felt a little bad for her, because he knew she would have to relive the events of the day by explaining them yet again. But based on his time with her and her family, this round would probably end up being the easiest and would bring the most healing. While Emily had a great relationship with both her parents, she had a very special bond with her dad. She could always talk to him, and he was a good listener; it was part of who he was.

Emily's father, Simon, was a prosecuting attorney working in the office of the Assistant District Attorney (ADA) downtown. Emily theorized that he had become such a good listener because his job required him to absorb everything that was said to him. But she also theorized that he was probably never going to advance to become District Attorney because of his sense of fairness and honesty. She figured that, to get to that level, you needed to be able to bend rules and occasionally look past things to get your man—something she knew her dad could never do. Regardless, Emily was very proud of him, whatever his occupation.

He worked very hard and often worked late, but rarely worked on Saturdays, which was kind of a bonus. Most weekends, the family had 100 percent of his attention; but this weekend was different. Something was going on …

"So, Em … what happened today?" he asked.

"Oh Daddy, do I have to tell this horrible story again?" Emily whined pathetically back at him.

"Well, I got some of it from your mother already—" He paused. "But I'm going to need to know everything. Otherwise, these things can snowball into some real ugliness." He smiled at her reassuringly. "*And* I really need to know that you're okay."

Emily slumped down onto her bed and gathered herself before starting. "Jen and I were driving to the mall after the SAT this morning, and I got a text … and in the split second that I tried to look at it, this woman stepped out onto the road, pushing her baby stroller …"

Emily's dad listened intently, occasionally nodding to convey his understanding of the facts, but looked down at the floor throughout most of the story. Emily laid out the facts, calmly and clearly, and as emotionally upsetting as the whole event was, Otium could see that she was feeling a little more relief as she recounted the event for him. When she finished, there was a long silence between them. Her dad just continued to stare at the floor.

Otium often found it very difficult to watch the people in his charge make mistakes, so he could only imagine how it must be for a parent. He could see the pain and concern all over Simon's face, as he relived the events of the day through Emily's words. At the same time it was very obvious that he was relieved that his little girl was not in the hospital, and would not have to live with the heavier burden of her actions being the cause of ending another person's life due to a few moments of irresponsibility. Simon was taking his time to choose his words and react in the best way he could to help his daughter learn from this mistake, while reassuring her how happy he was that she was okay.

"Daddy," Emily sweetly whispered.

"Yes, sweetheart," he replied.

"Are you angry at me?" Her voice cracked just slightly, as she began to well up with tears.

He paused for just a moment and then earnestly said,

"Sweetheart, you made a mistake, and I'm just glad no one was seriously hurt!" He pulled her in for a hug once again. "But I still think there need to be some consequences."

Emily nodded, still clinging to her father's embrace. "I understand," she whispered.

"What do you think is appropriate?" Dad sat back a little so he could see her eyes.

"Maybe—I should be grounded?" Emily said slowly.

"Go on ..."

"Grounded from the car?" she suggested halfheartedly.

"Go on ..." he said again.

"From my cell phone?"

"Yes—and your friends." He spoke softly, but with strength. "I think, one month on the car and cell phone. Three weeks from your friends."

Her eyes widened as she realized that his "sentence" overlapped with prom, which was in two weeks. She looked at him and tried to hold back the tears.

"Does this sound fair?" he asked.

"Daddy, prom is in two weeks. I have my dress already"—she motioned to her dress hanging on the closet door. "And John just asked me to go."

"Oh." He paused thoughtfully. "With all this commotion, I guess I missed that big news. When did he ask you?"

"Just a minute ago..." Emily said excitedly, then realized what she had just said.

Uh-oh, Otium thought. This could be a tough one. She had just gotten grounded, and now she was going to have to come clean on the events of the last hour. Otium moved to sit down next to her across from her dad.

Emily's Dad cocked his head to one side a little, kind of like a dog hearing an odd noise. "So he called you?"

"Not exactly," Emily said slowly.

"What do you mean?" Her father knew he was on to something. "You said just a minute ago ... Was he here?"

It was Emily's turn to study the floor, unsure of what to say.

She knew she was in trouble, and now she would have to admit to new offenses. And although she was not a liar, pressure had a way of making people morally malleable, leading them to actions they would normally not consider.

Otium leaned into her ear and slowly whispered, "Truth." To Emily, it sounded like a word whispered on the wind. She looked up and scanned the room.

He knew she had heard him. He leaned into her ear again: "Truth …"

She looked down again and began explaining, "He came over here … He climbed up the tree and into my window …" She was speaking quicker and quicker, as only a teenage girl is capable of doing: "I told him he wasn't allowed in my room, and he was only here a few minutes—just long enough for me to tell him what happened. He was worried. That's why he came to see me."

Emily's dad shook his head, and then looked up to the heavens, still shaking his head. "Emily—what am I going to do with you?" he said, exasperated.

"I'm sorry, Daddy, it won't happen again! It was a mistake. I wanted to see him … and then he was here, and he was soooo sweet." Emily was again quickly explaining. "This was a onetime slipup, Daddy. I promise it won't happen again!"

Emily's father sat silently staring again at the floor. He looked a little angry this time, but was definitely weighing the facts and circumstances.

Otium could never be a parent, as it was not part of his nature (as a Seraph), but he again wondered what it would be like. He had observed so many generations of families and all it entailed: conception, birth, growing, learning, training, finding a spouse, then having one's own children, raising them, and so on. He was never jealous of humankind, but parenthood was such an awesome gift. It was very special, and yet very difficult. He sat on the edge of his seat, waiting for the verdict. It seemed like hours. Simon sat there, silent on Emily's bed, thinking…

"Daddy," Emily said, in almost a whisper.

Finally he spoke, standing up abruptly. "I'm glad you were

honest with me, Emily. I'm sure it was tough, and I'm glad you told me the truth." He paused again. "You can go to prom—"

Emily sprang up, excited and joyful. "Thank you, Daddy, thank you for understanding. It won't ever happen again, I promise!" She was practically jumping up and down.

Her father stopped her, grabbing her by the shoulders, and calmly said, "Emily, we have rules like no boys in your room for a reason. At your age, or for that matter at any age, things can happen really quickly, and once they do, you can't easily take them back or change them. Look at the accident today. In your own words you said you 'looked away for a split second,' and look what happened."

He paused for a moment, thinking hard about what he wanted to say. "Don't get me wrong, Emily. I trust you, your mom trusts you, and someday you'll see that it makes sense to have rules and enforce them on yourself, whether it's about a budget or who you'll date. But right now, it's our job to establish the rules for you until you can do it yourself."

As Emily listened, she calmed down and became more serious. "Daddy, I understand. You are right," she said, looking seriously into his eyes. "It's just like that kiss from John—it came from out of nowhere, and happened about as quick as the accident did—"

"Kiss?!" Simon exclaimed, raising his voice in shock. His eyebrows shot up so high on his forehead that they seemed to disappear into his hairline.

"Oh!" Emily anxiously blurted out. "I forgot to mention that … It was no big deal, Daddy! Probably less than two seconds long …" Emily explained nervously, speaking incomprehensively fast, while combining her best "innocent smile" and wincing a little at the same time.

Simon stared at Emily with a frozen expression of shock for a long moment. Finally, he shook his head as if recovering from a splash of ice-cold water on his face.

"Okay, I just want you to think about what happened today and learn from your mistakes. Now go to bed. I'm sure you're bushed!" He hugged her tightly again.

"I love you, Daddy," Emily said with a muffled voice, as she buried her head into his shoulder.

"I love you too, sweetheart. Get a good night's rest," he said, forcing a smile through the look of shock still on his face. Then he released her from his hug and pointed out the window to "John's" tree as he walked out of her room. "Tomorrow, we're going to be trimming some tree limbs away from your window!"

Chapter 12

EMILY SAT ON HER BED with her calculus book and homework pad open. She had not made any progress for at least forty-five minutes. She sat there, pencil in hand, staring at the same unsolved problem. Overall, she was taking her punishment well and didn't try to fight it, but the grounding did seem to have led to more daydreaming.

Otium felt a little helpless, but he knew that this was one of the necessities of life. Some times when you mess up, you have to suffer the consequences. And while some people seemed lucky and got away with more than most, usually things eventually caught up with them.

Strangely enough, the ones who were receiving help from the other side to beat the odds and escape the consequences, usually felt the heavy backswing of the pendulum worse than if natural justice had reached them on its own. The dark ones loved to give extraordinary help to help people succeed in the short term, because they loved even more to yank the rug out from under them later. Not because they had some kind of moral code or desire to seek justice or balance, but because once they built someone up, it made for a grander fall.

The simplest (human) prey for demons to entice were always the lazy ones, mainly because they were always looking for shortcuts. It was easy to influence them, because they were always wanting to get something for nothing. For example, the gambler types; all it took were a few winning hands to build a false sense of confidence. Before long they'd be laying their kids' college fund on the table, only to have it blown on one wrong card. Meanwhile, the fiends would be invisibly gathered around, giggling like schoolchildren. Ruining those lives was so easy, it was like shooting fish in a barrel.

Emily's cell phone was vibrating again. Otium looked over Emily's shoulder as she picked it up to see who it was.

Jen was texting her again.

She stared at the phone, and Otium could tell that she was weighing the pros and cons of opening the message and responding to it.

The curiosity must be killing her! he thought.

Emily was able to see Jen at school, but with the exception of lunch, school severely limited their prom planning time together. They were in many of the same college prep classes, but they were on different schedules, so they had them at different times. They really needed to talk; there were many little details that needed to be worked out regarding the prom, and part of the fun was the planning. The only other time they could talk was during their elective soccer class, but they were usually running around most of that hour, making conversation problematic.

She abruptly threw down her phone without looking at the text, obviously frustrated.

She is trustworthy, Otium thought.

How many kids would have just peeked already? Her parents would probably never know. But Otium knew that this was not her style; she would do her very best to honor her parents' wishes, even down to the simplest detail. This was one of the reasons that he really enjoyed this assignment.

Her phone was buzzing again. She picked it up and glanced at it again. This time John was calling. This was going to be really tough.

She took a long hard look at the phone.

"Argh!" She moaned loudly before jamming the phone under her pillow. Suddenly, there was a light tapping at her door.

"What now?" she moaned.

"Emily?" It was her dad.

"Oh, Daddy ..." Emily jumped up to answer the door. "I'm sorry, I just keep getting calls and texts. I can't get anything done. I've been staring at the same calc problem for like an hour—"

"You haven't been answering them, have you?" Simon asked.

"No, Daddy."

"You know, you're not supposed to be even using that phone," he lectured. "You should probably just shut it off!"

"I know, Daddy, this has just been really tough ..." Emily complained. "Jen and I just have a lot to talk about with prom coming up—and I'm sure John is just trying to make sure his tux matches my dress. There's so much to—"

"Yeah, yeah ... I hear you," her dad interrupted, "but I'm not letting you off."

"Daddy," Emily said sweetly, "you didn't even let me give you my sales pitch!"

He just glared at her, and Otium could literally begin to see his blood pressure rising. Generally, he was a very patient, calm man, but in this case, Otium figured he was still smarting over the fact that a young man had climbed into his little girl's bedroom. The question now was whether Emily would just be wise and back off, or if she would continue down her current path. Wisdom was such a tough skill to learn!

"Don't push your luck, Emily!" he growled, as he turned to leave the room.

"Daddy?" Emily said, just as sweetly as before. "I was only messing with you. Did you need something?"

He abruptly stopped walking. "As a matter of fact, I do."

"What is it? Whatever you need!" Emily purred.

Uh-oh, Otium thought, smiling to himself. She was starting to lay it on pretty thick, and her dad was a pretty sharp guy.

"Well, I don't think I could ..." His voice trailed off. He was also laying it on thick as he drew her in to call her bluff.

"Daddy," Emily interrupted, standing up and putting her hands on her hips and brightly smiling. "Absolutely anything you need!"

"I could use some help at the shelter this Saturday," he finally said.

"Gotcha!" Otium said out loud to himself.

Emily's smile faded quickly. "Daddy! Some of those people creep me out!" she exclaimed. "Please don't make me do it!"

"Creep you out?" He was now visibly annoyed again. "Emily Grace! You should be ashamed of yourself!"

Emily said nothing, but her body language said volumes. She quickly looked down, she was a little surprised at herself this time.

Otium leaned into her ear. "Just do it," he whispered.

"Emily, we have so much," he said, lowering his voice. "But I'm not going to guilt you into this—"

"Daddy, sometimes I'm just not good with people," Emily explained.

"Offer to help without the people part," Otium whispered in her ear again.

"That's fine, just forget it," he said as he started to leave again.

"What can I do where I don't have to *be* with anybody?" Emily said quickly.

Emily's dad turned around again, looking thoughtfully at her. "Hmmm ..." he said. "That's not a bad idea. There's always a ton to do. I'm sure we can think of something ..."

"Great!" she exclaimed, relieved to somehow find some common ground with her dad.

"And I don't suppose you know any doctors or nurses who would be willing to put in a few hours too this weekend?" he half-seriously asked.

"What?" Emily said, crinkling her nose. "I thought you had a doc that was volunteering."

"We did, but he backed out," he said with disappointment. "Something about liabilities and lawsuits ..."

"Did you tell him you knew where he could get cheap legal counsel?" Emily asked earnestly.

"Yeah, I actually told him I would represent him for free if anything happened." He shook his head in disgust. "I think he was just looking for a reason to back out."

"I'm sorry, Daddy," she said, taking his hand. "I'm sure you'll find someone else to pitch in."

"I hope so. There are so many people who need help, and health care has gotten so expensive." Both of them quietly contemplated their last few statements. Emily could see on her father's face what Otium could feel in his spirit: that Simon was genuinely saddened that he could not do more to help.

"Well, anyway—we leave at six," he said abruptly as he turned and walked out of her room.

Emily paused in shock for a moment, contemplating whether his comment was a joke. "Ha-ha!" she half teased. "You're so funny."

"Not joking …" he said over his shoulder as he continued down the hall.

"Crap," she said under her breath. "I'm sure even homeless people sleep in on Saturday."

"I heard that!" her dad shouted, now out of sight.

Emily plopped back on to her bed, shaking her head. "Six a.m. on a Saturday—that doesn't stink at all," she murmured sarcastically to herself.

Chapter 13

OTIUM SAT ON THE LARGE industrial-size refrigerator in the shelter kitchen as the volunteers buzzed around him like bees. There was something uplifting about watching them busily go about their tasks. It made him feel a little more at home, since so much of his life was dedicated to service. Some of the volunteers were professional chefs, while others were just regular unskilled folks helping out around the kitchen, but everyone had something in common: they were all happy to be a part of giving a helping hand to those in need.

Then there was Emily, still working on cutting the same small bag of potatoes for at least the last half hour. It was almost laughable to Otium, and for fun, he started counting her yawns. Thus far, twelve yawns to seven sliced potatoes. *Oh well, at least she's here,* he thought.

Then her dad bounded in, checking on everyone's progress. "Come on, people, we've got to get moving!" he cheerfully announced. "The kitchen will be opening for lunch in about an hour!"

"Hey, Simon … I think the bottleneck is in the potato dicing department!" Maurice teased (one of the more portly professional chefs). Then, walking over to Emily's station, he announced,

"What kind of potato soup are we going to be able to make with these six measly potatoes?!"

"Seven potatoes!" Emily quickly sassed back at him, playfully sticking out her tongue.

"I think we need to send Sleeping Beauty back to bed," Maurice said with a chuckle, "she's a wee bit cranky today!"

Emily raised her fists mockingly, as if taunting him to fight. Holding his hands up as though to surrender, the much larger man backed away, now laughing hysterically.

"Okay, Emily," her dad said, joining the fun, "let's give the potatoes a rest. I think we had better hand that job off to someone else. Otherwise, our lunch will become dinner."

Just as the laughter began to die down, one of the staffers from the administrative office led someone into the kitchen. "Emily, you have a visitor!" she pleasantly announced.

To Emily's surprise, it was John, and what started as a pleased and excited greeting turned into a very awkward moment. "John!" Emily exclaimed, smiling, while gritting her teeth. "What are you doing here?"

"Well, I was in the neighborhood, and it looked like one of the windows was open, so I just climbed right on in!" John joked, without realizing that her father was standing right next to her. Emily's eyes became as wide as saucers, and she quickly gave John the universal signal to knock it off by moving her outstretched hand back and forth across her neck.

"Daddy," she said, turning toward her dad to make introductions, "this is John, a good friend of mine from school."

John's expression changed abruptly, and he quickly shot out his hand to shake hands with Simon. "Hello, Mr. Newhouse, I'm John. I'm a friend of Emily's from school," he said, nervously.

"Yeah, I think she just said that," Simon replied, locking eyes with John. He then deliberately took an extra moment to make John squirm as he waited with his outstretched hand, before finally extending his own hand to John. "And I know who you are. I spent all last Saturday trimming tree branches because of you," he said in a very serious tone. Then he turned to Emily. "You realize you are grounded even while you are working here?"

"Yes, Daddy," she replied, again trying to turn on her sweet charm.

"Mr. Newhouse," John interrupted, "Emily didn't know I was coming. It was my idea to stop in. I just thought maybe I could volunteer for a couple of hours, and still get to spend some time with her too."

"Aww, that's really sweet," Maurice interjected with another chuckle.

"Maurice, can we have a minute?" Emily's dad shook his head, trying not to laugh.

He looked down, considering what he should do next. Otium had seen many father-to-boyfriend interactions, and this had the potential to go either very well or very badly. He knew that taking a stand at the wrong time sometimes ended up pushing the young lady away and directly toward the boyfriend. He wondered if this was what Simon was considering right then as well, and if he wasn't, he was surely doing an effective job at making Emily and John very uncomfortable as they waited for his response.

Finally, Dad said, "Okay."

Both John and Emily let out a huge sigh of relief, smiling at one another.

"Excellent!" John blurted out. "I think we can really help out here!"

"Thank you, Daddy!" Emily exclaimed, nodding in agreement with John.

"No problem," her dad responded, as he led them to the janitor's closet. "I think I have just the job for the two of you; requiring quite a unique set of skills!!!" Opening the closet door, he handed a toilet brush to Emily and another to John.

Otium busted out laughing, while eagerly anticipating Emily and John's response.

Emily and John just stared at their brushes, silent, and then looked at each other flabbergasted. "Daddy, are you serious?" Emily said, in shock.

"You said you were looking for a job where you could help out and didn't have to *be* with anybody," her dad retorted. "And

I'll tell you what, if you guys do a good job, I'll let you have the afternoon off—together."

Emily suspiciously narrowed her eyes. "You'll suspend my grounding?"

"Yep, but just for today … and I want you two to head back toward home. This area is a little rough."

"You got yourself a deal, Mr. Newhouse!" John exclaimed, and then looked at Emily. "Let's get busy!" He grabbed two buckets and two bottles of cleaner.

"Yeah," Emily said slowly and sarcastically, while giving her Dad the stink-eye and trying not to grin. "Thanks a lot …"

"No problem. I love you, sweetheart." Dad said, as he crossed his arms smugly and winked at her with a big smile.

Chapter 14

ALTHOUGH OTIUM'S SPECIALTY WAS PROTECTION and battle, the Boss never pigeonholed any of His Seraphs. Otium had witnessed and participated in many different activities, varying from spectacular to sleep-invokingly mundane, and when he reflected on his life, they all had elements that he could consider "interesting".

This, he thought, *is one of those marked moments that I will remember forever.*

Of all the courtship rituals he had seen, some romantically sugar sweet, some distastefully aggressive, he had never seen a young man clean multiple toilets for the object of his affection. All while she supervised, endlessly talking on and on about what any other teenage boy would have classified as girlie-type subjects.

Emily sat on one of the sinks, swinging her feet back and forth as she talked on and on. First she told him about all the microscopic details of her prom dress, and then she told him about all the tiniest details of Jen's prom dress. Then she moved on to how Jen's date was unwilling to coordinate his tuxedo style and colors with her dress. Then she shared all the details that she had heard about from the decorating committee.

As the conversation went on and Otium witnessed the interaction, he began to feel more and more comfortable with

John. Infatuation was often a very strong motivation for a young man to tolerate a lot of things, but John did not appear to be tolerating anything. While Otium could tell he was not thrilled with much of the conversational topics or the fact that he was spending most of the morning cleaning toilets, he did seem genuinely interested in what Emily had to say. This made him "all right" in Otium's book.

As amusing as the conversation was, it was suddenly interrupted by the sound of breaking glass as a window high above one of the stalls shattered. Glass cascaded onto the floor, revealing a wire mesh that was meant to provide security to keep people out but could not stop them from vandalizing the window.

Otium was so absorbed in the spectacle of courtship before him that even he was surprised. Emily abruptly stopped talking, and the two of them looked at each other for a moment, unsure what they should do. From outside they could hear several young men laughing and talking, but they could not make out any words.

Emily quickly and carefully went to the stall under the broken window and motioned for John to follow her. They both stood silent, straining to listen to the jovial conversation outside, but could not quite hear any details.

"Boost me up!" Emily whispered to John.

"What?" he said, giving her a quizzical look.

"I want to peek out the window!"

John looked at her for a moment and then finally conceded. "Okay."

He was not especially athletic or coordinated, but after a few very awkward and scary moments of unbalanced struggle, Emily was on John's shoulders and straining to peer through what was left of the window.

"What can you see?" John whispered.

"Looks like a little gang of three guys … lots of tattoos, kind of scary looking," Emily reported, scrunching up her face like she had just eaten a lemon.

"Anything else?" John asked, as he readjusted himself, straining to keep his balance.

"Stop moving around!" Emily scolded him, almost falling off sideways.

Otium thought it was going to be mostly a non-event until he heard the familiar voice of her father outside.

"Hey, you guys—beat it!" he yelled. "I saw what you did to that window!"

"What window?" the apparent leader of the gang shouted back, and then they all started chuckling.

"Come on now, guys, we're just a homeless shelter," Simon reasoned. "We don't have money to spare on broken windows."

Otium peeked his head through the wall just in time to catch one of the punks rushing up to Simon to give him a start. With him was one of the dark ones—one who looked familiar to Otium, but he had not yet formally met.

"I said ... *what window?*" the leader yelled, throwing his hands up in the air. Simon flinched and stepped backward. "Are you coming into my neighborhood and accusing me of breaking *my own stuff?*"

Emily nearly fell off John's shoulders as she clambered to get down. "Oh no!" she cried. "John, we've got to help my dad! They're going to beat him up!" And she raced out of the restroom.

Otium passed through the wall and took a stance next to Simon.

"What is this about?" Otium commandingly questioned the demon.

"Otium, what a great honor," he mockingly replied. "I have always wanted to do business with you directly someday!"

"Sorry, I don't think I know you," Otium shot back, "and honestly, I'm really not interested in making any new friends today."

The demon smirked as he sized up Otium for just a moment. He was lanky but looked formidable, with piercing black eyes and what looked to be sharp talons extending from his forearms, which he was attempting to tuck out of sight behind his back. He then turned his gaze to Simon like he was prey, while he continued his conversation with Otium.

"I am Acerbus, and every day since Micmash, I've wanted to"—now he looked back slyly at Otium—"meet you."

"Micmash?" Otium responded. "You were there? There with the Philistine army?"

"Yesss," the demon hissed, circling behind the gang member who charged Simon. He whispered something into his ear, and then addressed Otium, "Excuse for an army, is more like it... Hairless apes! Cowardly ... hairless ... apes they were!"

It was the first time that Otium had worked directly with Cidem. Cidem was assigned to Jonathan, the firstborn son of King Saul and heir apparent to the throne of Israel. Jonathan was like a modern-day rock star or sports icon. He was tall and handsome, commanding the pick of any woman in Israel. But like superstars of the twenty-first century, he could be reckless and impulsive. He and his armor bearer had crossed through a pass between two mountains and were making their way up a hill toward the enemy Philistine camp, when the Boss sent Otium down to assist Cidem.

Cidem was lying in the grass next to Jonathan when Otium arrived and greeted him warmly.

"Hello, Otium, I am very happy to see you," Cidem replied. Motioning to Jonathan and his armor bearer, he said, "I think I'm going to be very busy in about two minutes and could really use your help."

"So what's the plan here?" Otium asked, lying down in the grass next to the armor bearer.

"I don't think there is one. I think Jonathan just decided to—" Cidem was interrupted by the two men suddenly jumping to their feet and charging up the hill. He immediately sprang into motion and waved for Otium to follow.

"Otium, you take the armor bearer, and I'll stay on Jonathan!"

Both young men were charging toward a group of twenty soldiers manning an outpost at the edge of a bigger camp. The Philistines began taunting Jonathan, as he and his bearer charged forward; they were obviously not taking this threat very seriously. After all, it was two against twenty …

Jonathan drew his sword and expertly hacked through the first soldier he encountered. His father, King Saul, was a conquering warrior king, and as his son, Jonathan had been well trained in combat skills from boyhood.

The armor bearer was another story.

As he rushed up to his first opponent, his combat stance practically screamed, "Come, chop off my arms!" Instead of being tucked in close to his body for protection and control, his arms flailed loosely as he swung his sword wildly about, paying no attention to whether he was attacking with the edge or the flat of the blade. After observing for a moment, Otium decided to take charge before the man cut off his own arm or leg.

Standing behind the young man and grabbing both his wrists, Otium began guiding his motions. Pushing him forward to duck, then to parry, then slicing through opponent after opponent. Within minutes the skirmish was over, and only the two Israelites were left standing.

"What the heck, Cidem?" Otium said, turning to Cidem. "What is going on here? What's with these two?"

"I know, I know," replied Cidem, laughing and waving his arms. "Jonathan decided to pick a fight! And off he ran, right into this mess … He was telling his bearer all about how the Lord would deliver them, and off he went!"

"Did the Boss tell you this was the plan?" Otium asked.

Cidem shrugged. "You know He doesn't tell us everything. Sometimes He talks directly to them too. Maybe He told him to attack them?"

"I don't know, but apparently He approves, or He wouldn't have sent me!" Otium declared. "And by the way, it's great to finally work with you." He extended his hand toward Cidem with a smile. But before Cidem could accept it, they realized that Jonathan and his bearer were off running again. Running toward the bigger camp.

Otium and Cidem flew after them, and as they approached

the main camp, Otium began counting the tents. "Cidem... what are we going to do? There's more than two hundred tents here. They cannot take on this many soldiers alone!"

"I know," Cidem replied. "And look—" He pointed toward the camp. There were demons everywhere.

"What are we going to do?" Otium asked Cidem earnestly, as they continued after Jonathan.

Cidem looked up and whispered, "Abba?"

He did not have to wait long for an answer. Nodding while still looking upward, he answered the Boss, "Okay, got it!"

Cidem then blurted out, "Otium! Follow me!" And he blazed off toward the camp, passing Jonathan and his bearer as if they were standing still. Passing through the first tent, he began screaming and yelping at the enemy soldiers. They couldn't see Cidem, but they could feel the sudden force ripping through the tent as he passed through it and hear his horrifying shrieks. Startled and terrified, the soldiers ran outside the tent. Cidem did the same to another and then another.

As the men ran out of their tents, they were confused and ran into each other. As Jonathan and his bearer ran into the camp, they easily began hacking and slicing their way through their ranks. Otium followed Cidem's lead and began screaming and yelping as he sailed through the camp as well. That's when he saw the pack of demons gathering a short distance off, organizing themselves to attempt an attack.

Otium yelled to Cidem, "Follow me! We've got to counter them before they organize and attack!"

Otium shot off toward them, flying as fast as he could. Ducking his head into his shoulder like a linebacker, he plowed into a group of them, scattering them like bowling pins. Cidem was close behind and crashed through a second group, and as they ricocheted in every direction they slammed into the hilly ground and nearby trees. The earth shook, and the Philistine troops panicked even more.

Seeing this, Otium looked at Cidem, and they both immediately knew what to do. Grabbing one of the dazed and fallen demons by the arm, Otium swung him around like an Olympic hammer thrower. He spun around with the demon four times before finally releasing him in a trajectory straight into the ground. Cidem grabbed another demon and did the same, and as both angels took turns slamming their evil brethren into the ground, the earth trembled. With each hit, it was as if a mighty earthquake had struck the site.

Otium's flashback was interrupted by Acerbus shouting, "You ruined me! You and your pal! I was in charge at Micmash, and because of that debacle—I'm stuck with these morons!"

The lead gang member grabbed Simon and shoved him into the shelter wall as his two henchmen moved to either side, trapping him between them and the wall. Otium stepped back and prepared himself for battle. The situation was deteriorating fast, and this demon had a score to settle.

"Get away from him!" Emily screamed, as she came around the corner, flanked by John.

The initial expression on the gang member's faces was one of surprise and shock. Laughing, the leader turned back to Simon saying, "What is this? Some kind of—" He fell silent as five of the men from the kitchen rounded the corner just behind Emily and John. Each of them brandishing a kitchen utensil as a weapon.

"Back off!" boomed Maurice, waving a giant frying pan in the air.

At first the gang stood motionless, as though in shock, as they sized up their competition. Slowly they started to back away from Simon, as they each concluded that getting whacked with a frying pan was not an enjoyable proposition.

"Go on, get lost—*losers!*" John yelled, surprising Emily as well as both sides of the assembled mob. He was not the most commanding man there, but she sweetly appreciated his effort. She rushed up to her dad and threw her arms around him.

The gang leader shot John a look that probably would have made him lose bladder control under other circumstances before turning back to his group. "Come on, Players. This is a joke." The gang backed away and exited the shelter lot.

"You will get yours, Otium!" Acerbus snarled, gritting his teeth. "Kako told me that the Lord shines on you every day, but mark my words"—he moved in closer, going eye to eye with Otium—"someday it will be cloudy, and *you will get yours!*" Then he spun on his heels and quickly followed his gang out of the lot.

"Wow!" Simon exclaimed to Emily and the kitchen group. "Thanks a lot. I thought I was going to get the snot kicked out of me!"

"You were!" Maurice teased, laughing. "But fortunately for you, you got a tough little girl who saved your butt!"

"I certainly do," Simon responded, hugging Emily tightly.

"And John helped too!" Emily exclaimed.

"We would have never known what was going on, if it wasn't for her!" Maurice said.

"Really?" Simon asked, pulling back a little to look into Emily's eyes.

"Yeah," Emily said, faking an attitude. "We were cleaning the restroom where they broke the window! It scared the crap out of us!"

"At least you were in the right room for that!" Simon said jokingly.

"Ha-ha! Very funny!" she mocked.

"Well," Simon said, cocking his head to one side and slyly looking at her through the corner of his eye. "I think you've earned time off for good behavior!"

"Awesome!" Emily shrieked.

"Let's get the heck out of here!" John exclaimed.

Chapter 15

THE WEEK FOLLOWING THE INCIDENT at the shelter was relatively uneventful, especially by recent standards. Otium had not seen or heard from Kako, but this was not too unusual. In the past he had gone decades without interaction with Kako, and then suddenly he would be back in his face. His absence suited him just fine.

Since Emily was still grounded, she spent every free second at school making plans with Jen and generally talking nonstop about the prom. Now the big day had arrived, and she and Jen were sitting luxuriously in chairs at the salon getting their hair, nails, and makeup done. All their preparations were leading up to a double date for the prom.

It was an exciting time for Emily, and this made Otium happy. All Seraphs loved human-kind, but the bond between angels and their charges always ran very deep. They were not always assigned for an entire human's lifetime but always during some important period of their lives. Sometimes it was because of some turmoil or trial where they needed help, sometimes it was to help the Seraph grow through partnering with their human; but it was always somehow related to carrying out the Boss's plan. And during that time, the Seraphs would grow very close to their humans. Otium thought it must be like the bond between protective older siblings and their younger brothers or sisters.

In the meantime, the break in the action gave Otium time to think and reconnect with the Boss too, and the communion with Him refreshed his being, just as much as it re-centered him. Otium had concluded that all beings needed time to recharge and that that refueling occurred via different methods for each of His creations. For his kind, regeneration was obvious and natural due to their direct linkage to the Boss. The nature of the way they were created drew them to Him, and as His conduits to the world, their connection to Him was perfect. After spending time in His presence, Otium always felt that his mind and being were sharp and he was once again ready to take on the challenges assigned to him.

Otium watched as the stylists worked on Emily and Jen, applying curlers and chemicals to their hair. The girls seemed to really enjoy the transformation process, possibly more than they did actually seeing the final result. It was all rather curious to him, as he did not have a physical being to maintain, and he was now as he always had been from the day when he was created. His "appearance" was not related to working out, clothes or styling; it was manifested via His Glory, not from anything Otium did.

I guess this is just another way they recharge, he thought. *Kind of inefficient and temporary, though …*

For humans, it was pretty different. While many had found God, they didn't have the same kind of perfect connection, so the replenishment was imperfect. That was why He gave them spouses and family and friends and hobbies—to help fill in the gaps. The problem was that too often, just like the Expelled, they would become so focused on what they could do for themselves and what they wanted, that they would become like addicts. Doing only what was necessary to fill themselves up and no one else.

Emily and Jen's conversation suddenly became interesting, drawing him out of his philosophical trance.

"Do you know where they are taking us for dinner?" Emily asked.

"No, Chris wouldn't tell me," Jen replied, giggling.

Jen had been completely giddy ever since she had accepted Chris's invitation. He was, after all, either the captain or the star varsity player for just about every sport their school had to offer.

"Jen, I have to tell you," Emily said, trying not to hurt Jen's feelings. "I hope Chris behaves tonight. He can be a bit of a jerk sometimes."

"I know, I know … and an egomaniac and rude, but I think he's really coming around. And"—Jen paused and looked around—"he is soooo *hot* too!" She giggled.

"Oh, give me a break!" Emily said, exasperated.

"*He is!* Haven't you seen him in that tight little wrestling outfit? He looks like a Greek god! I'll bet you just about anything that he ends up in the movies or as a model or something…"

Emily rolled her eyes. "What-ever …"

"You know he rented a limo, don't you?" Jen replied.

"Really?" Emily scrunched her nose.

"Yup! I think he really wants to make this really special. That's why the boys aren't telling us where we're going for dinner. They are trying to be sooo ro-man-tic!" Jen said, raising her voice an octave in her excitement.

"Romantic, huh? You really think so?" Emily questioned, as she wasn't quite buying it. "You know, all that romance might be smoke screen for his real plan."

"I know," Jen said playfully, "but it doesn't mean that I have to cooperate—unless …"

"Jen!" Emily shouted. "Don't you dare even think it! Don't waste yourself on *him!*"

"I know, I know," Jen replied with the slightest bit on condescension.

Emily just shook her head, half disgusted with her best friend.

Wow! Otium thought. He had not seen this side of Jen before, and this did surprise him. Simultaneously though, he felt a wave of pride run over him after listening to Emily try to coach her friend. Something told him that tonight was going to be a very busy night!

Chapter 16

"O... M... G!!!" JEN EXCLAIMED. "I don't think I've ever eaten so much!" As she climbed back into the black stretch limousine as the driver held the door.

"It was incredible!" Emily chimed in. "I think you guys have to let us pitch in; it was way too expensive."

"No, no ... Emily, it was absolutely my pleasure!" John persisted, slumping down next to her in the luxurious leather seat.

"Going to this place was worth it, if only to see Jen jump ten feet into the air when the lobster on the presentation tray started moving!" Chris teased, as he took his spot next to Jen on the bench seat facing Emily and John.

The limo drive stuck his head in the door. "So it's off to the hall then, right?"

"Yes, my good man—and don't dilly-dally! We don't want to be late," John said in his best English accent. The girls giggled at his silliness, while the driver just rolled his eyes and responded, "Yes sir."

It was a wonderful evening, Otium thought, relaxing on one of the open bench seats. He had seen many, many impressive meals, and this one definitely ranked within the top five, but there was quite a range between number five and what would have been number one in his book. No one did excess like the Romans.

Then again … there was that crazy King Ludwig in Germany too. He could really put out a spread!

"I think this gesture of our generosity and romanticism must deserve some type of reward," Chris suavely suggested, leaning in close to Jen's face.

"I think you are right, handsome," Jen said seductively, leaning into him as well.

Just as Emily began to feel a little uncomfortable, Jen slipped to one side and gave Chris a giant lick up his cheek!

He lunged backward. "*Gross!* That's not exactly what I had in mind."

As John and Emily laughed, she turned to him and delivered a sweet peck on his cheek. "It was a marvelous dinner!" she said in her own fake English accent.

"Anything for my lady," John said, echoing with his terrible but cute accent and reaching for her hand, smiling from ear to ear.

Otium sat and watched in amusement. They were being silly, but sometimes being silly was perfectly all right. After all, it wasn't very often that regular folks got to indulge in expensive meals and limousines.

"Emily," John said, suddenly taking a more serious tone, "have you decided on what you are going to do about college?"

"No." She sighed. "I've applied to a few now, but I don't know what to do."

"That's an easy one," Chris interjected. "You're so smart! You can do anything. You should just pick the thing that will make the most money!"

"Yeah, right, Chris," John shot back. "It's that simple."

"It is," Chris reasoned. "Once you got the cash, all your worries are behind you. It's easy to be happy then!"

"I had no idea you were such a philosopher," Jen joked.

"You can't be serious," Emily replied, sounding disgusted.

"Don't listen to him, Emily," John retorted. "I just think you should go for whatever makes you happy and makes you feel good about yourself."

They all went silent for a moment after John's serious declaration, taking long looks at one another. Then Chris blurted out, "Okay … Dad!" and punched him in the chest. And they all started to laugh while making themselves a little more comfortable for the rest of the ride to the hall.

Finally when Chris and Jen appeared to be distracted in their own little world of nonsense, John turned back to Emily. "I was just curious. I didn't mean to throw a wet blanket on things."

"You didn't, John." Emily paused, touching his cheek. "I just can't make up my mind."

"I just want you to know," John said, looking into her eyes, "I hope you pick a school that has a great computer science program…"

"What?" Emily said quizzically. "Why?"

"May be you're not so smart after all." John laughed, shaking his head. "Because that's going to be my major …"

"Oh—" Emily laughed, then smiled broadly, finally realizing what he meant.

"How absurd," Kako grunted, suddenly sitting next to Otium. "They are like gnats mindlessly buzzing around—although I do think I like this Chris fellow …"

"You," Otium sighed. "What do you want?"

"You always sound so disappointed to see me," Kako mocked. "By the way, I heard you and Lothario hit it off famously. I knew you'd like him."

"You mean that 'Casanova demon'?" Otium shot back at him. "You never told me that your kind were environmentalists. Did he tell you I helped him to realize that he was really a tree-hugger at heart?"

"Very funny, Otium. I thought you had enough sense to mind your manners and treat a guest with respect, and then you threw the poor fellow out on his ear! And for what? He was just trying to encourage a little love in this unkind world. It's a wonder that

I make an effort at all to carve out time for our special little visits, with you being so cantankerous all the—"

"Don't pretend like you're here because you care," Otium interrupted him. "You're here to make trouble, but I'm telling you right now, I'm not going to let you."

"Aww, come on now, Otium, do you really think that little of me?" Kako replied innocently.

"Actually, yes," Otium retorted. "You're a troublemaker, and I'm not going to let you ruin their evening!" Then he grabbed Kako by the shoulders and held him still as the limo passed transparently through them and continued onward. They stood in the middle of the highway as cars raced by and through them.

"What are you doing?" Kako yelled at him. "How dare you! Since when do you strike first?"

"Since now!" Otium shouted back.

"Now?" Kako cocked his head to one side. "What has suddenly changed?"

"I've just been thinking a lot lately, and I decided that you're not worth it," Otium declared sternly. The two glared at each other for a moment.

"What does that mean?" Kako asked.

"Exactly what it sounded like. I used to think that if I showed you compassion, you would change your mind and give up on this Rebellion. I used to think that if I was patient and put up with your garbage, you'd come around—but I was wrong!" Otium yelled.

"You were trying to convert me? You were trying to bring me back"—Kako looked puzzled and stuttered a little—"back into the Light?"

"Yes. But I realized that would never happen. You think of no one but yourself, and for some sick reason you enjoy causing pain and hurting people. You don't want to come back, and you don't deserve to anyway!"

The two stood on the freeway, just staring at each other. Otium was angry, and finally out of patience. He stood ready, and this time Kako would not surprise him. He would not let him suddenly cause an accident or trip someone or make someone feel bad. This time, Otium would not allow himself to be stabbed in the back.

"Unbelievable," Kako hissed, shaking his head with contempt, as he floated into the air and began to glide away. "You are pathetic and a moron, Otium. You had better go check on your girl!" And as suddenly as Kako had appeared, he was gone again.

For a moment, Otium felt satisfied. All the frustration he had harbored against Kako for all the times he had wronged him and the innocent people around him had been released with just a few words. Taking a deep breath, Otium reflected on the moment and began to get an eerie feeling; nothing with Kako was ever that simple.

Why did he tell me to check on Emily? he thought, as panic began to rush over him. His eyes widened as he realized that this could be a trap. He turned and, with all the speed he could muster, blazed down the highway toward the limo.

Chapter 17

OTIUM FOUND THE LIMO PULLED over on a side street near the highway. The hood was up, and steam was pouring from the front of the engine compartment. He assumed it was some sort of radiator problem, until he got a little closer and could see that this was not the result of natural causes. Two little "gremlins" sat giggling on the engine, as the stinky radiator steam shot out all around them.

Otium peeked into the back of the limo and found it empty. Emily, Jen and their dates were gone, along with all their personal items, and he began to fear the worst as he overheard the driver speaking with the limousine company.

"Yeah, I warned them, but they didn't want to wait, so they took off," the driver reported. "They thought it was only another mile or two … Yeah, I have to pick them up afterward, so I'll need another car."

Where are you? Otium thought, as he closed his eyes and focused, reaching out to find Emily's spirit. For a moment all he could see was darkness. Was he being blocked? Then suddenly it all became clear, and he could see her walking about a mile ahead. He opened his eyes, hovered gracefully into the air, and then shot like a bullet toward their location.

"My feet are killing me," Jen whined. "Chris, can't you carry me the rest of the way? I'm sure it would be a great workout!"

"Yeah, right. In my tuxedo? I don't want to get all sweaty and ruffled up," Chris complained. "And we're still probably two miles away!"

"What? You said we were only about a mile away when we got out of the limo!" Emily angrily retorted at Chris and then lowered her voice. "And this is not a great area …"

"Aww, come on, Em. This is South Bend, not Detroit or New York. We'll be fine," Chris replied, trying to act like the area didn't bother him.

Emily shot him a stern look. "Chris, my Dad works in the ADA's office, and he would have a fit if he knew we were walking around here. He told me this neighborhood sends him a lot of business."

Otium arrived just in time to witness, as though on cue, the three gang members they had encountered last week at the shelter, plus an additional two rounding the corner. This time all five men were in full gang gear, with matching bandanas representing their solidarity. But their fashion statement was the least of his concerns: this time, Acerbus had brought along two more demons on his mission.

Chris, in all his self-absorbed glory, plowed right into two of them, sending them stumbling off balance. Before realizing what he had done, and a little too instinctively, Chris snapped at them, "Watch where you're going"—His voice trembled a little as he realized what he had just done—"… buttwipe …"

While Chris was physically larger than any member of the gang, he certainly did not intimidate any of them. As much as he tried to keep his composure, they could smell the fear on him. One of the two he plowed into was a stocky man with slicked back, jet-black hair; and a large tattoo of a skull with a dagger stabbed into its head on his forearm. The Skull guy grabbed Chris by his arms and shoved him into the brick building behind him, restraining him against the wall. "What did you say?" he snarled.

Chris's cool-dude attitude is not going to get him very far with this crowd, Otium thought as he rolled his eyes and turned his attention to the dark ones.

"Looky what we have here," the smallest of Acerbus's friends said, stepping forward and eying Otium and then Emily and Jen.

"I knew this was going to be a great evening," Acerbus volunteered, smiling maniacally from pointed horn to pointed horn.

"Not only will our pupils get a little more street cred, beating the crap out of some well-to-do suburbanites," the last and largest of the three demons said, while slamming his fists together, "but we'll get a chance for some sparring practice with the great Otium!"

"Gentlemen, apparently my reputation precedes me, as you seem to know me, but I am really only acquainted with your wise and skilled leader, Acerbus," Otium said sarcastically, rubbing salt in that old wound. "I am always up for a little sparring, as your kind needs as much practice as it can get—but these kids are nothing to your little gang," He reasoned while chuckling a little, trying to lighten the situation. "These young ones are hardly a match for your band of so-called warriors. Let them pass."

The demons erupted with laughter, except for Acerbus, who fumed with animosity and revenge toward Otium. Acerbus moved to position himself beside two of the gang members closest to Emily and Jen and then whispered into the ear of one of them. Like a mindless robot, he all too obediently began to slowly walk toward Emily.

"Yes, you are right, they are nothing," the little demon hissed. "Just a little warm-up for the evening … kindling for the fire," he said as he slithered over to one of the men Chris bumped into and whispered in his ear.

Otium had recognized the big one as Allirog from long, long ago. He was quite a skilled warrior, and like some sort of freak of nature, he had two pairs of powerful arms. If this came to a confrontation, Otium knew he would have his hands full just handling him, let alone all three of the demons at once. He watched cautiously as Allirog moved to place himself directly between himself and the girls, puffing up his chest like a silverback gorilla, trying to intimidate Otium.

"This is not happening," Otium growled, looking into the black eyes of Allirog. "You will leave here in pieces before I let you touch them!"

John stepped forward with his hands up, trying to defuse the developing "human" situation. "Come on now, guys, we really don't want any trouble. Chris didn't mean it, he just wasn't paying attention … he's really just a dumb jock with a big mouth."

"Wait a second—you're the little punk from the shelter parking lot last week!" the gang leader said, stepping up to John and crossing his excessively tattooed arms.

"What did you call me?" he demanded, giving John a really scary stink-eye before continuing his interrogation. "What was it? Loser? What do you think you're in some kind of a movie here, sport?"

"We don't want any trouble, Sheriff …" another of the gang mocked in a fake nasal Southern accent.

John looked at Emily, and it was clear that he didn't know what to do. The girls were backing themselves into the alcove of a closed store entrance as two of the gang members continued to move in, effectively blocking their only exit away from the danger.

Suddenly, Chris lost his pseudo composure and yelled, "You guys had better just back off!" He pointed at Emily. "Her dad is like a cop!" Chris yelled, squirming his way out of Skull's grip and falling down hard to the pavement.

"Shut up, Chris!" John yelled.

"You guys mess with her, and you'll be sorry!" Chris continued.

Acerbus perked up. "Oh, this is bad news for you Otium…"

"These guys get extra points if they can mess up a cop," the little demon giggled sinisterly.

"Family members are just about as good as the cop themselves," Allirog added.

Chris scrambled to his feet and started running, surprising the Skull and his partner. The two ran after him without even considering why, if only to catch him and beat the tar out of him. The little demon went after them, laughing wildly and shouting to the others, "Once they catch him, I'm sure I'll have to coach these primates on what to do with him. I'll catch up with you later!"

Things are escalating too fast … I've got to slow things down, Otium thought. He focused hard on John to send him a message: *"Calm down …"*

John was looking back and forth rapidly at the gang members and then to Emily and then back to the gang. Otium could see that he was scared and starting to panic. Unfortunately, the remaining gang members could see it too.

"Calm down!" Otium transmitted hard, trying to reach into John's mind.

One of the three remaining men stepped forward and grabbed Emily by the throat. "So your dad is a cop?" he growled.

Jen began to meekly whimper, "Just leave her alone... please..."

"He's just a lawyer... in the DA's office," Emily bravely shot back at him, struggling, grabbing at his hands and trying to pull them away from her throat.

"A lawyer? You mean a prosecutor, right?" He slammed her hard against the wall behind her, still maintaining his grasp on her throat.

Otium looked at John and could see that he had had enough. This guy was grabbing his girl, and he had to do something. John suddenly let out a very theatrical-sounding karate yell: "Hiiiii-yahhhh!" His fists were up, and he was in some kind of a fighting stance that he had probably seen in a movie.

"Uh-oh …" Otium sighed out loud. "Here we go."

Chapter 18

ALLIROG USED JOHN'S DISTRACTION AS an opportunity to lunge at Otium. With two hands he grabbed Otium's throat, while using his other set of hands to capture his sword arm into a joint lock. As Otium squirmed to get free of him, Allirog suddenly began to sprout another set of arms, which he used to grab at Otium's free arm. Allirog was a powerful demon, and he had tied Otium up so that he couldn't grab his sword.

Moving swiftly, Otium shifted his weight, using his free arm to strike the demon three times in rapid succession—first to the face, then the gut, then the face again. The sudden trauma stunned Allirog enough that Otium was now able to break his sword arm free, but ...

Acerbus charged forward pouncing on Otium's back, and grabbing his head, he began shaking it violently. Acerbus was like some kind of wild animal, and he began to extrude long sharp talons from his forearms. Preparing for a deadly strike, he wound up, raising one of his taloned arms into the air. But before he could plunge it into the back of Otium's neck, Otium grabbed it with his free arm, keeping Acerbus from driving it into his body.

As Otium struggled to keep the two demons at bay, he glanced anxiously at Emily and John, wishing he could help them as their conflict heated up as well, but he couldn't... He was more than occupied.

The gang leader took one look at John after his karate yell and with a laugh, he stepped forward and planted his foot firmly on John's chest, delivering a powerful lunge kick. John flew backward, like a ragdoll, eventually slamming into the wall behind him and knocking the wind out of him. Falling to the concrete, and gasping for air, he struggled to get back to his feet.

Simultaneously, Emily's captor began to repeatedly slam her against the wall, still holding her by the throat. "Stop! Stop!" she protested, in a raspy voice, due to his grip on her throat. But he didn't care; her pleas were falling on deaf ears. Then he wound up and delivered a heavy backhand across her face, knocking her to the ground next to John.

"God ..." she desperately whispered, with tears running down her face, "please help us ..."

Emily's whisper was like a shout in Otium's ears. He looked up to the heavens and himself called out, "Yes, Lord ... help us ... *Help me!*"

With that, Otium immediately began to feel himself surge with heavenly Power. Glancing at John, who was now barely standing, Otium could see with his consecrated vision a Powerful glow developing all around him as well.

Intending to finish John off, the gang leader took another step forward and wound up for a knockout punch, aiming to land it squarely on John's jaw—but John suddenly moved, dodging the blow. Instead of John's face, the gang leader's punch landed solidly on the brick wall behind him, shattering most of the bones in his hand. The leader fell to his knees in immense pain, clutching his now useless hand.

John, suddenly re-energized with Heavenly strength, moved to position himself between Emily and her assailant, bravely intending to protect her from any additional abuse. As John prepared to square off against the man who had struck "his" woman, the gang member that was occupied with Jen turned his attention to John after witnessing his leader's failure to take him out. John wound up and swung his fist wildly, delivering what could only be described as one part uppercut, one part right cross, and two parts haymaker—landing it exactly on target, into the nose of Emily's foe. He screeched in pain, snapping his head back violently as blood gushed from his face, and unintentionally head-butting his buddy (Jen's antagonist) behind him. Both assailants were taken completely by surprise and stumbled backward in complete disorientation, holding their faces in pain.

Upon seeing this incredible chain of events, Otium suddenly realized that he was now free of the burden of worrying about Emily, Jen, and John and could turn his full attention back to dealing with Acerbus and Allirog.

Allirog was again attempting to get a grip on Otium's free arm, and it was then that Otium realized their strategy: Allirog's job was to hold their victims still, while Acerbus would tear them to pieces with his talons.

Still holding onto one of Acerbus's talons, Otium began to twist it away from himself, angling it toward Allirog, and with one quick jerking motion, he reversed the force he was using to fend off Allirog. Instead he abruptly pulled Allirog toward him and right into Acerbus's razor-sharp talon.

The talon plunged deep into Allirog's chest. Screaming, Allirog frantically pushed Otium and Acerbus away from him as a foul stench sprayed out of the open wound. He began staggering in circles, deliriously clutching his chest, in excruciating pain.

With Allirog off him, Otium could now focus completely on Acerbus. He yanked him off his back and flung him to the ground. Acerbus rolled across the ground, and sprang up into a fighting stance, baring his talons toward Otium. Otium drew his sword, and it glowed brightly like the sun, causing Acerbus to squint his evil eyes as he hissed, "You are nothing, weak and unfocused ... I'm going to cut you to pieces!"

Acerbus leaped forward to pounce on Otium, but he was ready and sliced the attacking arm and talon cleanly off. Acerbus crumpled to the ground, shrieking in pain and clutching the socket where his now missing limb had been attached. Standing ready, Otium stood over him, poised to put down any counterattack, but none came. Acerbus instead just lay on the ground, rocking himself back and forth as he tried to deal with the immense pain from the amputation of his arm. Both beasts were beaten.

Neither demon approached again, but neither did they retreat at once. Allirog wandered around the area for some time, holding his chest and crying in pain, but eventually his random wandering took him farther and farther away from the scene. While Acerbus just lay on the ground seething with anger, cursing at Otium in some demonic language, reeling with pain and quite done for the evening.

Finally Otium could again turn his attention back to the kids.

Two of the gang members had already left the scene, leaving a trail of blood from their faces behind them, while the gang leader just sat on the ground, staring at his rapidly swelling broken hand. And in the middle of it all, John was now holding Emily, sweetly, his body bent over her as though he were shielding her from the evil of the world.

As Otium walked toward them, he thought, *I really, really like this kid.* He smiled. *He's not much of a warrior, but he got the job done.*

"John, I can't believe this," Emily sobbed. "This was so horrible!"

"It's okay now," John calmly comforted her. "It's all done now. We'll just call a cab and go home."

"I thought prom was going to be the best night of my life ..."

"I know, me too," John said but then abruptly stopped in midsentence.

Otium saw it happening, but it took him by surprise, and he stopped dead in his tracks.

Emily looked into John's eyes, and something looked very strange ...his eyes began to water and she could see the veins began bulging on his forehead and around his neck as he slumped heavily forward onto her.

"Emily," John said, letting out a very deep breath.

Then she saw it—a knife stuck out of John's back. The gang leader had stabbed him, just before he cowardly fled into the night.

"Jen!" she hysterically shrieked. "Call 911!"

Chapter 19

OTIUM WATCHED AS THE PARAMEDICS worked feverishly to stabilize John. His injury was obviously quite severe, and Otium wished that Cidem could have been there to tell him just how serious it was and how he could help. The only thing that Otium did know was that the next few hours would be crucial. Otium could see that the knife had damaged John's spinal cord, and the paramedics did not even want to attempt to withdraw the blade, deciding that it would be better to leave that to the hands of a skilled surgeon.

Emily and Jen were desperately holding onto each other a few yards away, sobbing, as the first officer on the scene tried to extract as much information from them as he could about the gang, and specifically their leader. The girls were trying to respond to him, but much of it was coming out as half-formed thoughts and phrases, and sometimes just gibberish. The girls were too upset to communicate anything worthwhile or useful, and the sight of John on the gurney was too upsetting, even for Otium.

It is all so confusing for them, Otium thought.

The evening had began so wonderfully, with fancy dresses and handsome tuxedos, leading up to a spectacular meal, then ending in this tragedy. And while he had seen many tragic events and a lot of suffering that he didn't understand; Otium always took comfort knowing that somehow it *always* worked out according to the Boss's Plan.

It was a little easier for him as an angel, not because he knew any more of the Plan than what had already been revealed to humanity, but because he could see so much more of the puzzle coming together. For example, Emily and John could not see the series of vicious spiritual battles that had occurred prior to this, that ended up being the catalyst to the physical conflict between them and the gang.

Yet even though he trusted the Boss, something didn't sit well with him about this encounter. Had he been set up by Kako? Or was this just the result of Acerbus's lust for revenge? And regardless of the motivations or schemes, how did this fit into the Plan?

This was the confusing part for Otium. God gave the gift of Free Will to humans and angels, and this meant that He allowed things to happen, because if He didn't, then there would be no true choice, no real freedom to choose a path. But what did God want him to do now? Was there more to this event, more to happen?

Suddenly Otium realized that Kako was standing next to the ambulance, watching Emily climb in after John was loaded for his transfer to the hospital. Otium raced over to him. He was angry, angrier than he had ever felt before. And the emotion swelled up inside him and like a volcano, he was ready to erupt.

"What are you doing here!?" he shouted.

"I heard what happened," Kako condescendingly replied, "and needed to take a look for myself—just like gawking at the scene of a serious car accident. Especially after the way you dismissed me earlier ..."

"This is your fault!" Otium screamed, clenching his fists.

"What are you talking about? You're the one who was away from your charge," Kako mocked. "Could you imagine if I hadn't clued you in?"

"Clued me in!?" Otium raged back at him.

"I was helping you. You were in the middle of dressing me down on that crappy freeway—" Kako paused. "Maybe it's more accurate to say you were *judging* me on that freeway, telling me how worthless I was, and then I just reminded you of your true job …"

Otium was so angry that he had difficulty reasoning through Kako's premise, and his hands shook as he struggled to deal with such strong emotions. Was he judging him? He looked away and thought hard about the conversation. His words were very harsh, and he did say mean things, but he spoke the truth.

"You were so condescending, so mean … I thought—I thought you were …" Kako paused and then a wide, evil grin spread across his face. "*Me!* I didn't even do anything, at least not today, and there you were talking down to me. Is this your God's love in action?"

Otium looked into Kako's eyes. Was he actually right? Otium felt more confused than he'd ever been. If he was acting like Kako or his kind, then he was wrong. He didn't ever want to behave like them.

Long moments passed as the two stared at each other. Otium felt paralyzed by his confusion, and finally his good nature and desire for forgiveness took over.

"Kako, you've done so many horrible things in the past," he stuttered, lowering his voice. "I was just so sure that you were there to cause trouble again. I'm sor—"

"You are pathetic," Kako quickly interrupted. "Look how easily you are swayed!"

Kako hovered into the air, just a few feet away from Otium. "You want so desperately to change my mind. Do you honestly think that I want to be like you?" Kako shouted, laughing and again mocking him. "What's wrong? Don't you have any friends? Are they all so pathetic and weak like you, that you want to recruit one?"

"What?" Otium said, stunned and confused. Kako was doing it to him again. Leading him down one path, and then turning on him, only to attack him.

"Of course I planned this, you wuss!" Kako screamed. "So what are you going to do about it?" Then he blasted into Otium, almost knocking him down, as he raced off like a bolt of lightning across the sky.

Otium stood stunned for a moment in disbelief. His fear was true. Kako had effectively thrown Emily and John's lives into complete chaos, all while he had stood by trying to "convert" him. He had neglected his duties, dealing with this scum, giving him a chance. Otium felt angry again. Very angry.

"Enough is enough!" he shouted and raced after Kako.

Chapter 20

I AM NOT GIVING UP. I will catch him, and this will end, once and for all! Otium thought, slowly gaining on Kako.

Each time Kako changed course, he would momentarily pause just long enough to check if Otium was still in pursuit. The chase continued for several hours as the two shot across the sky like a couple of shooting stars, traveling faster than humankind would define as possible.

Kako led them to all the ends of the earth, from deserts to the depths of the ocean, through office buildings to remote Arctic ice plains. Suddenly he stopped, high above the earth, just long enough for Otium to get very close to catching him.

"You're not getting tired, are you?" he yelled, laughing and taunting Otium. "At the very least you are a persistent idiot!"

Otium said nothing in response. He knew that he was not the fastest of his kind, while Kako was a speed demon of sorts, so he stayed focused on the task at hand: catching him, making him pay.

Finally, Otium got close enough and grabbed hold of Kako's foot. Yanking him to a hard stop, he wound up to deliver a hammer blow that Kako would soon not forget. Kako looked shocked and unbalanced, as he suddenly realized that he was caught, and his taunting smirk of a smile turned to fear.

Otium slammed his fist into Kako's chest, sending him spiraling back to Earth, like a fighter plane that just got shot out of the sky. He watched with satisfaction as Kako tumbled out of control and tried to stabilize himself.

"Your kind has no place in this world, or anywhere else for that matter!!!" Otium bellowed, shaking his fist. *"You'll never win!"*

Kako finally regained control and turned back toward Otium. There was pain on his face, but he yelled back at him, *"Is that all you've got?"* Then he shot off in another direction.

Otium reengaged pursuit. *This must be the last time,* he thought. *This must stop!*

He did not want Kako to hurt one more person, and this needed to be their last battle.

Kako began slowing over Haiti, in a dark, heavily forested area, and Otium could see that there was some sort of gathering where he was setting down. Otium landed a few feet from him.

"Kako, this needs to end," he declared. "Over the millennia, you have hurt hundreds and ruined thousands of lives, and I can stand for it no longer—"

"Yes, yes … Otium, this does need to end, and when this is through, you will not have to stand for it anymore." Kako slowly and venomously hissed. "This is our realm. Earth is ours … and you have no authority here."

Otium cautiously surveyed his surroundings. The blood of chickens had been sprayed everywhere, and the natives, thoroughly spattered with it, were engaging in some sort of voodoo ritual. Some were jumping around chanting and moaning, while others were in a trancelike state. They were calling upon a power they didn't understand, a power that, if they had known the truth, they would want no part of.

"These people know the truth," Kako hatefully lectured. "There is power here, power they can access, and with that access they can do what they want. They don't need to follow any silly rules or codes of conduct or honor."

Dark ones began appearing from out of the darkness all around

Otium, demons of every kind. He began counting them … five, eight, twelve … and then he lost count. There were too many.

"You are right about one thing, Otium: this will be the end," Kako shouted, "the end of you!" Kako then raised his arms, directing the demons toward Otium, rallying them to attack.

That's when Otium realized the trap he had fallen into. He went for his sword as at least a dozen lunged toward him. Even in the darkness of this place, he sword gleamed like a beacon of hope, blinding some of the hoard as they charged.

Otium swung with precision, slicing the first to reach him cleanly in half. The halves of his body flew violently into the trees with such force that the trees were uprooted, stunning the natives. As the evil one's spirit dissipated into nothingness, even the people present could hear his scream. Confused and terrified, they scattered like a colony of ants whose hill had just been trampled, as the spiritual battle began spilling over into their physical world.

There were too many opponents for Otium. Three jumped on his sword arm as countless others piled onto him, biting, scratching, digging talons and claws into his belly and back. No sooner would he fling one of them off than another would take its place. As Otium skillfully spiraled around, fighting frantically to beat off the hoard, he knocked over trees, people, and whatever else was in the way. Through it all, he could occasionally catch a glimpse of Kako, who did not engage but just stood and watched as they overwhelmed him.

With the demons swarming on him, he lost his footing and crashed to the ground. Again the earth shook as they piled on top of him. They began to pound on every part of his back and head, pounding him into the ground, and as they did, the ground continued to quake.

Slowly Otium was slipping away as the darkness overwhelmed him, and he was too bruised, too beaten to fight any longer. He stole one last glance at Kako, who was still standing just a few feet away from him.

He still isn't participating—why? This was his triumph, wasn't it?

Otium's eyes felt heavy, and there was nothing left, nothing he could do... he was beaten...

In finally desperation, Otium uttered one word, "Abba ..."

Suddenly all was still and there was silence. Absolute silence, for only a second.

Then all Otium could see was light, a blinding, overpowering light—and the demons began shrieking. The sound was deafening, it was as though someone had poured acid on all of them simultaneously. Otium struggled to lift his head and could see them being caught up in a whirlwind, being thrown in every direction ... their bodies disintegrating as they spun.

And then, as quickly as it began, it all stopped. But the light remained.

Otium felt the healing warmth pour over his body, as he was enveloped by his Father's love and power, helping him get back to his feet. Kako was the only demon remaining.

God's voice filled their heads: "This is over. It is time for you to go, Kako. Tell your master what has happened; tell him your plan has failed."

Otium could see the fear in Kako as their eyes locked for a moment. Then Kako was gone.

Chapter 21

"THANK YOU!" OTIUM GRATEFULLY EXCLAIMED. "Once again you have rescued me, once again you have restored me ..."

Otium smiled as he felt his Lord's love enveloping him, healing every part of him.

"Otium, what were you doing?" the Boss's voice echoed in his head.

Otium hesitated to answer, as he knew that there were no real questions for the Boss; He knew everything. He knew everything that had happened, and everything that was going to happen long before it did. He was not asking because He wanted an answer, He was asking because He wanted to reveal something.

"Kako has been hurting them for a long time," Otium explained, "and I guess I finally just had enough."

"You'd had enough?" He questioned.

"Yes. I have just been thinking about all the times I tried to talk to him—tried to get him to understand why he made the wrong choice—but ultimately things would always somehow end with him lashing out at me. Or at them, just so he could get to me," Otium continued.

"So were you upset because he hurt Emily and John?" He continued His inquiry.

"Yes," Otium replied, but as he did, he realized that it was more than that. He felt hurt and betrayed because every time he had reached out to Kako, his compassion was repaid with pain. He felt hurt that he would try to trust Kako, only to be stabbed in the back in return.

The Boss knew all these things; He could feel what Otium was feeling and understood it. "I understand your pain, Otium. I have been betrayed many times Myself … but there is something more, isn't there?"

Otium stood quietly as he searched his feelings. There *was* something more: the anger that had pushed him to take matters into his own hands. "I was angry, my Lord," he slowly replied.

"Yes, you were. Why were you angry?"

Otium could feel the emotions welling up inside him again as he thought of everything that had just transpired. "I was tired of the pain, the betrayal—" He paused. "I showed him kindness! I tried to bring him back home! And he spat in our faces …"

As Otium continued, he felt the anger was building as it did before. "I guess I'd just had enough and decided that *we* would be better off without him."

"Otium"—the Lord spoke slowly but sternly—"you just said 'We.' I do not remember being consulted."

"Lord, he is vile … he is despicable," Otium earnestly explained. "I just thought getting rid of him was the right thing."

"So you decided to end him?" the Boss patiently asked.

Otium lowered his head. "Yes …"

"In your anger, *you* decided to end him," the Boss pressed on, emphasizing each word.

"It seemed like the right thing, Lord," Otium reasoned. "Your vengeance is *always* just …"

"My vengeance?" the Boss questioned, even more sternly than before. "Was it My vengeance, Otium?"

"Lord—it was the right thing to do!" Otium protested.

"Otium, listen to yourself—" The Lord paused. He rapidly lifted Otium high above the earth and then instantaneously transported them to the nebula He had once created before him. "Do you remember this place?"

"Of course I do, Lord!" Otium exclaimed. "It was the most incredible privilege; and you chose me to be a witness!"

The Lord waved His hand, and immediately the gigantic cloud began to collapse in on itself, as a massive star began to form. Within seconds, all the dust was swept up into a brilliant ball of light and energy. "Otium, did you know that this was going to happen?"

Otium was stunned and confused. He had thought he was doing the right thing, but was he?

"Otium!" the Lord's voice boomed. *"It was by My will that this nebula was created, in my timing … and in my timing it has ended, and I manifested something else! Nothing is so big that it is beyond my reach, and nothing is too small to be unworthy of My care! It is I who decides how things begin and how they end."*

Otium fell before the Lord, bowing, realizing his error. "I am sorry, Lord!!! Please forgive me," he pleaded. "I was wrong!"

He felt the Lord's love all around him as he felt His hands lift him up, back to his feet.

"Otium." His voice was powerful but softer and loving, echoing in his head. "You have always been My faithful servant. You have carried out My direction flawlessly, and your heart always shines brightly with your love for Me and for My creation …"

Otium was suddenly returned back to earth, back to the site of the battle.

"Otium," the Lord said even more softly. "It was not enough for Kako to just trap you to kill you. The purpose of his trap was to lure you into stepping outside My Will … taking things into your own hands out of hatred and anger and doing things their way, not My Way."

Otium lowered his head, thinking back over everything that had happened in the course of the last few weeks. He had become completely wrapped up in all the specific events and in his own frustration over Kako's targeting of Emily. He had allowed his ego to become bruised, making him Kako's victim once again, and his anger clouded his judgment. In that state of mind, he stepped outside the Plan and acted without consulting the Boss.

“I’ve been such a fool.” Otium began to weep. “I played right into his hands … I’m so sorry.”

“ Yes, Otium … you were wrong,” the Boss said, in a gentle voice, with a proud smile. “And I forgive you, but you cannot let this happen again—you are one of my best and most trusted!”

“Thank you, my Lord,” Otium replied, as he felt the huge weight of his error lifting off his shoulders. “I will do better.”

“I know you will,” the Boss reassured him. “Our adversary is tricky and cunning. You must learn from this. Now, get back to work! There’s a young lady who could really use your support!”

Feeling completely restored, Otium shouted, “It would be my honor”—He paused, smiling from ear to ear—“and pleasure!”

Chapter 22

EMILY SAT IN THE HOSPITAL waiting room holding her head in her hands. With a throbbing migraine, she went through tissue after tissue. She had only just met John's parents a few hours ago for the traditional pre-prom photos, and the phone call to inform them that they were at the hospital was about as difficult as difficult could get.

They must have asked her a dozen questions, none of which she could answer, because hospital rules prohibited the staff from telling her anything, and this made her feel all the worse. At least there would be some relief in knowing that once they did arrive, the hospital staff would update them, and then she could finally get some news on John too.

Otium's heart broke for Emily as he entered the waiting room. Although other people were waiting, she was the only one that was all alone. Neither her family nor John's family had arrived. Others noticed the sad scene too, as it was hard to miss: a young lady in a blood-soaked prom dress at a hospital. It was like a scene from a horror movie. Yet no one said anything, either comforting or judging toward her.

Otium put his arm around her but didn't know exactly what to do. He could not read her mind, and since she was sitting so quietly and still, he couldn't extrapolate what she was thinking from her actions. Was she blaming herself? Was she just worried about John's condition? What *was* his condition? Would he recover? Finally Otium concluded that it was probably all of the above, and he just hugged her; closing his eyes and focusing all of his peace onto her upset spirit.

A doctor dressed in surgical scrubs briskly walked up to the nurse's station and asked if John's parents had arrived yet. Emily jumped up and ran over to him.

"Excuse me, Doctor?" Emily politely interrupted.

The doctor said nothing in reply, just glancing at her and then back at a chart.

"Doctor?" Emily asked again.

"Yes, miss, I'm Dr. Earbetrev. What can I do for you?" he replied, showing his impatience.

"Well, I came in with John Schuster … he was stabbed earlier," she began, nervously trying to sound like an adult, but her unconfident stuttering gave her youth away. "And I was wondering if—well, …"

"Miss—?" Dr. Earbetrev peered at her, clearly seeking her last name.

"It's Newhouse, Emily Newhouse," she replied.

Dr. Earbetrev looked her up and down for a moment. "You are not a relative and not married to Mr. Schuster. Therefore I cannot give you any information about his condition."

Emily stared at him for a moment, as tears welled up in her eyes.

"I just need to know what is going on!" she whimpered. "He got stabbed because he was defending me—"

Otium stepped up next to the doctor and put a hand on his shoulder. Then he leaned close and whispered, "Come on now … it's no big deal. Just a few things about his condition …"

The doctor paused for a moment, weighing the consequences. Then he took her by the arm and led her away from the nurse's station. As he looked back over his shoulder, the nurse sitting at the station shook her head like a mother ready to scold her child for misbehaving.

"The knife entered at about the middle of his lower back, severing some spinal nerve fibers," the doctor began explaining.

"At which vertebrae? L1? L2?" Emily jumped in.

Surprised, the doctor continued, "Very good, you have some foundational knowledge. Between L2 and L3. We are trying to repair the damage."

"Has he lost any feeling in his legs or his thighs? Will he be able to walk?" Emily questioned.

"Slow down, Ms. Newhouse, this is very delicate surgery … and honestly we may not know until he begins his recovery. Sometimes it's a matter of therapy too," Dr. Earbetrev replied, showing a bit of frustration, while he was obviously impressed with her knowledge.

Emily looked away as tears began to gather in her eyes again. "Will his spinal cord heal after the surgery?" she asked, already knowing some of the possible answers.

"Miss Newhouse, I think I've already said too much—" Then the doctor looked around, as though he was being spied on. "It sounds like you might already know that spinal nerve fiber does not exactly grow back like torn muscle tissue."

Emily began crying. She knew it was quite possible that John might not be able to walk again. "Okay, okay. Thank you, Dr. Earbetrev. Please just do everything you can. He's a really good guy … he doesn't deserve this," she said between painful sobs. Otium wrapped his arms and wings around her, putting her in an angelic cocoon.

For the first time, Dr. Earbetrev actually looked sympathetic. He laid a hand on her shoulder. "I will do my absolute best," he said and quickly turned to head back for the operating room.

Emily stood sobbing for just a moment, right where the doctor had left her before suddenly hearing a familiar voice behind her. "Emily?"

Turning quickly, she saw her mom and dad just entering the waiting room. "Oh Mom … Daddy," she said, starting to sob again.

Her parents both grabbed her together in a tight group hug.

"Is there any news on John?" her dad asked. But before she could begin to explain what she had just heard, John's parents rushed in the door and up to the nurse's station.

"We are John Schuster's parents," John's father declared.

"Yes, the doctor was just looking for you," the station nurse coldly and efficiently replied. "I will get him immediately," she said, picking up the phone.

John's parents looked around the waiting room anxiously, as they waited for the doctor to return. Finally they saw Emily and came over to her.

"Emily, have you heard anything? Did they tell you anything?" his mother asked.

"They told me a little, but they would not tell me everything," she responded, trying to pull herself together.

"Please—what's going on?" John's father pleaded.

Emily took a deep breath and suppressed her crying. "John was stabbed in his lower back… it is referred to as the lumbar region. All of the vertebrae in the spine are numbered, and the knife entered between L2 and L3. This area is where the spinal nerves connect to various parts of your legs and pelvis—"

John's mother burst into tears and turned away from Emily toward her husband. He held her tightly, but both were focusing all their attention on Emily's words. As John's mother began crying, Emily's mom began to cry as well, empathetically feeling the pain of another mother for her child.

Emily took another deep breath and continued, "The doctor would not comment on the extent of the damage to the spinal nerves, but I think he was looking for you for permission to do something."

John's father tried to fight back the tears as he asked, "Did he say if he would walk again?"

"He didn't say," Emily somberly replied.

John's father broke down as his wife buried her face in his chest.

Otium knew Emily wanted to say more but was holding back. He could see the emotions rising in her as she tried to keep her composure. Putting his hand on her shoulder, he whispered, "You can do this … Be strong …"

"Mr. Schuster, I'm not an expert on this stuff, but I've done a few research papers on the nervous system and some of the new advances. It's not like it used to be … They may be able to help John," she said, forcing out a slight smile.

Good job, Otium thought with an inward nod.

"And this happened while he was defending me … doing the right thing," she continued. "I'm sure God won't let his good deed go unnoticed …"

"Oh boy," Otium said to himself, shaking his head. "If only it were that simple."

Everyone stood quietly as Emily's words hung in the air. Otium could see the expression on Emily's face start to change as she wondered whether she should have said anything at all. They hardly noticed Dr. Earbetrev approaching until he was right on top of them.

"Mr. and Mrs. Schuster?" Dr. Earbetrev inquired.

"Yes," John's father replied.

"Can I have a word with you and Mrs. Schuster privately?" he said, motioning them away toward a little room connected to the main waiting room.

John's parents slowly followed Dr. Earbetrev toward a consultation room, as Emily fought the urge to follow. Her emotional strength gave way, and the tears began to flow again. Her father put his hand on her shoulder and reassuringly nodded. "You did good, sweetheart."

Just before entering the consultation room, Mr. Schuster turned to her and held his hand out. "Can you join us Emily? I'm sure John wouldn't mind."

Smiling through her tears, she took a quick glance at both her parents before rushing after John's parents. "Thank you, Mr. Schuster," she said, graciously accepting his offer.

Chapter 23

HOURS PASSED AS EMILY, HER parents, and the Schusters waited for news. John's parents had signed a number of waivers, authorizing continued surgical procedures, and Dr. Earbetrev had given no clues as to whether John would walk again. He had only said that he was trying to mend all the severed nerve fibers but was not sure if it was going to be enough.

Trying to distract Emily from worrying, her father finally spoke up. "I noticed you received quite a bit of mail today."

"I did?" she replied.

"Yes, I was a little surprised to see a packet from Johns Hopkins," he said with smile.

"Yeah, it looks like a really good school."

Mr. Schuster had been silent for hours, but suddenly he spoke up. "Emily, Johns Hopkins is one of the best universities around."

Emily nodded. "That's what I've heard."

"John was quite proud when he described you to us," he went on. "He said you were super smart."

"Thanks, Mr. Schuster," she said, smiling. "So smart I can't figure out what I'm going to major in."

"Well, Johns Hopkins has a lot of them. What were you leaning toward?"

She looked nervously at her mom and dad, seeing them perk up, waiting for her response. "Lately I've been thinking about medicine … or maybe biological research?" Emily said, half questioning her own response and hunching up her shoulders.

"Oh Emily, I think you'd be great," John's father replied, then turning to her dad. "Mr. Newhouse—"

Simon interrupted, "Please, call me Simon."

"Simon"—and John's father paused for extra emphasis. "You would have been so proud of your daughter, after Dr. 'Arrogant' finished describing the procedure to us in the consultation room. Sue and I were so confused with all his techno babble—"

"He was so aloof and cold," John's mom interjected.

"For Pete's sake! I've got an MBA, I'm not a doctor—and this is about our only child!" John's father exclaimed, showing his full irritation. "But Emily took it down a notch and explained everything in a way that we could both understand."

Emily began to blush a little as John's father recounted the story.

He continued, "And she asked the doctor all the right questions; all we had to do was listen. It was perfect for us."

"It's so difficult to have a clear mind when they're talking about cutting into your little boy," Sue emotionally interjected again.

"Well, Emily?" Simon gazed into her eyes. "Sounds like you may have found your major."

"Daddy, I know you mean well, but … can we talk about this later?" she asked sweetly.

Simon just nodded and proudly put his arm around his little girl.

Otium felt proud of Emily as well, as he had witnessed the exchange firsthand. Through the discussion she was able to hold it together and really helped the Schusters understand what the doctor was struggling to communicate. Maybe this was to be her niche. Maybe all this had happened to help point her in this direction. *After all, you need a little rain to make a rainbow.*

Another hour passed, and everyone was again silent, deep in thought or worry.

"Daddy," Emily whispered in Simon's ear, " I need to talk to you."

"Of course, honey," he whispered back and then stood up and addressed the group. "Emily and I are going to stretch our legs for a moment; does anyone need anything?". They all politely declined.

"Let's go find the snack machines," Simon suggested, and Emily quietly followed him down one of the hospital halls.

Once they were out of hearing of the others, she spoke up. "Daddy, I know who did this to John."

"What?" Simon exclaimed.

"Yes, it was the gang of guys we caught vandalizing the shelter last weekend."

"Holy crap. Are you sure?" Simon replied, stepping in front of Emily and grabbing her arms.

"Yes, Daddy," she said, beginning to cry again. "The guy who stabbed John was the gang leader from last weekend!"

"Oh my ..." Simon gasped, pulling her in for a tight hug.

The two stood for a few minutes, embracing in the busy hospital hallway.

Finally Simon spoke again, while continuing to hold her. "Emily, we're going to catch this guy. I promise you. I'm going to call in every favor out there, and we're going to catch him."

He began to pull out his cell phone, and Emily put her hand on his. "Thank you, Daddy," she said between sobs. "But for now, I just want John to be okay."

Simon nodded, putting his phone back into his pocket, and hugged her tightly again.

Otium decided that it was time to do some poking around and find out what was really going on with John. Saturday nights at hospitals always seem to be pretty busy, and this was no exception. As Otium walked ethereally through the various sections and rooms of the hospital, it was full of activity, but he needed to find the operating rooms where the serious surgeries were being conducted.

Finally he arrived at John's room, and it looked as though they had just finished closing him up. Dr. Earbetrev had just exited to the adjacent prep and scrubbing room, while the assisting doctors and nurses worked to clean John up and move him to his room in the surgical Intensive Care Unit (ICU).

"I'll be out talking with the family," Dr. Earbetrev said as he left.

Otium stepped up to John's bed and tried to take a harder look at his wound. He was lying on his belly and still had most of the surgical towels on his back around the area of the surgery. He looked hard at John's spine, trying to see through the layers of skin and muscle in an attempt to take a good look at the spinal nerve tissue itself. He could barely see what he was looking for, which was the biochemical electrical energy the spine used for communication. He couldn't tell whether the intermittent pulses he was seeing were the result of his novice skills, or whether the doctor had just been unable to repair the damage.

Frustrated, he quit looking. *I wish Cidem were here. He could tell if it was fixed or not.*

After a moment, he looked up as though he were under the open sky, praying, "Abba? Is this his destiny? I would never question Your Plans; I just hope he will be okay …"

Just as Emily and Simon had returned from their walk, John's parents motioned for Emily to join them; the doctor was ready to give them an update. As Dr. Earbetrev began to lay out the unknown and dire situation of John's condition to his parents, he seemed a little less confident. He praised himself regarding his expert surgical skill, but ultimately, as John's parents questioned him, he wasn't exactly sure John would walk again or whether he would fully recover. After a while, the doctor's words began to blur into the background as Emily closed her eyes and did the only thing that she thought would help. She began to pray, and although she didn't know it, she was joining Otium in his prayer for John.

Chapter 24

MONDAY WAS STILL A SCHOOL day, but Emily's parents more than understood Emily's reasons for skipping. John had spent the entire day Sunday sleeping, and Emily had heard through his parents that the doctor thought he should be waking up sometime today. If he did, the doctor would want to run a series of small tests gauging the extent of the damage; Emily did not want to miss it.

Despite the possible downside and bad news that could be coming, Otium noticed that Emily was upbeat and looking forward to getting just a few more answers. Otium, on the other hand, was not so sure that this situation was going to end well for everyone, but he reminded himself, "Keep faith in the Boss's Plan. It will all work out for good somehow."

When Emily arrived at the hospital, she had to wait to be cleared before entering the ICU. The hospital closely monitored and limited the number of visitors, and she had to be buzzed through. Nervously she walked through the silent halls, where all she could hear was the sound of her own footsteps and the various beeping devices monitoring all the seriously ill patients.

Finally she arrived at John's room and tapped lightly at the closed door. As she did, she wished she could just suck it back in as she realized that she had not brought any get-well balloons, stuffed animals, or plants—but it was too late to run and get something, as John's mother answered the door.

"Shhhh," she whispered, holding her index finger to her mouth. "He didn't know you were coming ..."

Emily quietly snuck into the room and up to John's bed. He was still a little groggy, but his eyes widened as he saw her there.

"Emily," he whispered, forcing out a smile.

"Hi, John!" she whispered back, with tears welling up in her eyes. "How are you feeling?"

"Like I got the crap kicked out of me," John joked, grinning a little.

"Well you didn't," Emily whispered, smiling through happy tears. "And think of all the street cred you've just accumulated. How many guys in the gamers chat rooms can tell their buddies that they got stabbed for real for their girlfriends?"

John chuckled and then winced. "Don't make me laugh; it still hurts."

"Oh, sorry ... sorry ..." She smiled, putting her hand on his, and kissed him sweetly on the cheek.

John's father put his arm around his mother and they smiled at one another, observing the sweet scene between John and Emily.

Suddenly Dr. Earbetrev burst in without knocking, and everyone simultaneously shot him the same look of annoyance, so much so that he actually realized his infraction.

"Well, good morning, everyone. Am I interrupting?"

"No, Doc," John joked in a raspy whisper. "I've been hoping I'd actually be conscious the next time we met."

"Of course. Well, I figured I'd better come by and see if I'd earned my big paycheck," the doctor joked back. But nobody laughed.

What a jerk, Otium thought but decided it would probably not be in good form to trip him. *Certainly not exemplary behavior for a divine being.*

Seeing that no one found his comments funny, Dr. Earbetrev

cleared his throat and continued. "I'd like to do a simple test with this reflex needle, to check your sense of feeling at various spots on your leg." He held up what looked to be a ballpoint pen, but when he clicked it, a little needle popped out.

"Okay, let's go for it," John said.

"Are you decent under there?" Dr. Earbetrev said as he grabbed the sheet on John's bed. "I'm going to need to poke you in your upper thigh first."

"I think I have boxer shorts on under my gown, but I'm not sure."

"Probably not," the doctor said as he carefully began to pull back the sheet. Winking at John, he said, "We'll be careful, though."

Exposing John's legs, he started with his left, lightly touching his leg with the pen-needle and looking at John for a reaction. "Tell me if you can feel this," he said.

"Yeah, no problem." John smiled as he looked around the room. Emily breathed a huge sigh of relief.

"Okay ... we'll have to circle back and do a little more reflex checking, but let's move on to the right leg."

The doctor circled the bed and touched John's right leg. Otium could see John's expression of happiness from seeing Emily and the positive reaction of his left leg start to evaporate as he realized he was not feeling the needle touching his leg. *Oh no,* Otium thought. *Come on ...*

"Anything?" Dr. Earbetrev asked.

Tears began welling up in John's eyes as he just stared at the doctor's hand moving around his leg, poking him. He said nothing.

Emily tried to keep it together but was feeling the tears welling up too fast for her to control. She glanced at John's mother, who also had a fearfully sobering look on her face. She turned her face away after meeting Emily's eyes for just a few seconds.

Frustrated, Dr. Earbetrev walked to the end of the bed where John's feet were and tried poking him on the bottoms of his feet. Looking at John's face, he repeated, "Anything?"

Tears began to roll down John's cheeks, and he silently shook his head.

Dr. Earbetrev clicked his needle-pen, slid it back into his chest pocket, and crossed his arms. He shook his head in disgust for a moment, and then decided to try again. But much to everyone's surprise, he wound up slightly, and slapped the bottom of John's foot with his hand.

John suddenly perked up. The pained expression on his face from thinking he was going to be somehow paralyzed, changed at once to surprise.

"Did you feel that?" Dr. Earbetrev said in a louder, higher tone.

John just stared at his foot.

Dr. Earbetrev wound up and gave him another hot foot.

"John?" Emily whispered.

"I felt that!" John shouted in his raspy voice, smiling at everyone in the room. *"I felt that!"*

"Well, all right! That's what I wanted to hear!" said the doctor, now smiling.

"What does it mean, Doc?" John's father asked.

"Well, I think it means he's going to be okay," said the doctor. "He must still have some nerve damage, but the fact that he has some feeling is very, very positive. I think with some physical therapy and time, he's going to be okay."

"Will he need more surgery?" John's mother asked, wiping the tears from her eyes.

"Probably not, unless Dr. Earbetrev missed something— "Emily blurted out, before realizing it was probably not her place.

"I didn't miss anything," Dr. Earbetrev retorted with a rather strong tone.

"I mean, sometimes it takes time for the nerve fibers to mend," she added, wincing.

"Yes, which is part of the reason for therapy. John may need to teach his muscles and nerves to work together again," the doctor said, a little less aggressive, but still sounding superior.

"Well … thank you, Dr. Earbetrev, you've done a fine job," John's father graciously offered, holding out his hand.

Dr. Earbetrev shook it, adding, "I was worried for a second there, but I knew it would all work out."

"It sure has!" John's mother added as she and Emily both lunged forward to give John a hug.

Chapter 25

AFTER THE MIRACLE AT THE hospital, Otium noticed that Emily had a renewed sense of focus and balance in her life. He couldn't tell exactly what was running through her mind, but he had seen it in her before, before the SATs, the college applications, and all the craziness of the last few weeks. It was a feeling of peace and purpose.

Every day after school, she visited John at the hospital and cheered him on during therapy. His right leg needed a lot of work, as the nerve connections to it had sustained most of the damage, but his left leg needed work too. And it was hard work: most of the time John was tired and sweaty by the end of the each session.

After her visits, she would hurry home, finish whatever homework she had, and then research various topics relating to spinal injuries. She had developed an impressive curiosity for any information she could find on the nervous system.

After three weeks in the hospital, Dr. Earbetrev finally signed off on John's release. And not a moment too soon: there was only so much daytime TV that a young man could watch …

On the day he was to be released, John had one last therapy session at the hospital before continuing treatment on an outpatient basis. As usual, Emily showed up … on time, but on this day, with a dozen congratulatory balloons.

As the therapist ran John through his excruciating rehabilitation routine, he teased Emily, "So did you mug a clown on the way here?"

"No, there was a little old lady bringing them in to her grandson, and I just swiped them from her," Emily said, playing along.

"Well that's not very sporting," he replied.

"You'd be surprised. She was on my butt all the way to the stairs … that's where I lost her."

"Well, I'm glad you won. We can suck the helium out of them later for fun!"

"Great idea!" she exclaimed.

John went on with his routine, and even though it required his intense concentration, he clearly noticed that Emily had something more on her mind that she was celebrating.

"So what gives?" John questioned, forcing out a smile as he struggled to walk between two balancing poles.

"What do you mean?" she asked coyly.

"I think you know what I mean," John shot back playfully.

"Yeah, I guess there is something on my mind …"

"Okay, well, let's have it!" He looked up, taking a break from his exercise.

"I've finally made a decision." She paused. "It's something that's been on my mind for weeks …"

"Come on Emily! You're killing me here!" John said, feigning annoyance.

"Okay, I've decided to go to into medicine!" Emily grinned. "I'm going to try to get into Johns Hopkins!"

His jaw dropped as he heard the news, but in hindsight it was pretty obvious to Otium. All the pieces were falling into place, and as terrible as the events of the last few weeks had been, they collectively came together to spell out a message to Emily: that she valued people, that she could really make a difference, and that she had the brains to do it. Usually Otium was good at connecting the dots, but with all the turmoil caused by Kako, this one went completely over his head. Yet this young lady got the message.

"John's Hopkins?" John paused. "That's in like... Maryland..." As much as John was smiling, it was obviously forced. He was happy for her, but didn't want her to go.

"Yeah!" she exclaimed. "Isn't it exciting?"

"That's great news," he said, still smiling as he went back to his exercise.

As he continued, there was a long silence between them. No questions, no joking, none of the usual silly banter. The excitement and smile slowly faded from Emily's face.

Otium had seen many plans fall apart, as couples disagreed over future directions. It would be a shame if Emily was reconsidering her decision based on John's mixed reaction.

"John," she said sweetly.

"Yeah," he grunted as he continued exerting himself.

"You know—" She coyly paused again. "Johns Hopkins has a great computer science program."

John stopped his exercise and stared at her for a moment, evaluating what she was suggesting.

"Really?" John said as he began to smile brightly.

"Really!" Emily emphatically nodded back.

He hobbled over to her and pulled her into a giant hug.

"Johns Hopkins it is," John declared. "If they'll have me ..."

"Awesome!" Emily exclaimed, hugging him tightly.

End Of Volume One